"You see my _____,
earrings, and _____,

"and you automatically think I must be with Doberman, a skate rat who goes around terrorizing guys like you on the boardwalk."

Danny nodded. "He sure acted like you were together."

"Looks can be deceiving, Danny."

"You have a tattoo?" Danny asked.

Raven nodded.

"Where? Or aren't I allowed to ask?"

She looked at him slyly. "You can ask. Who knows if I'll tell? I wouldn't want you to get the wrong idea about me."

"What idea is that?" Danny asked.

She popped a wheelie with her board and slammed the front end down with a loud *whap*. "That I'm a drug-doing, class-cutting, mosh-pitting sleaze who likes to hang out in the backs of vans at Nine Inch Nails concerts."

"You mean you aren't?" Danny chuckled. "Darn."

Raven tried to keep a straight face, but a smirk crept through.

of dyed pink hair, to long ... and my hair?" Raven said.

Brothers Trilogy

Danny

ZOE ZIMMERMAN

BANTAM BOOKS
NEW YORK · TORONTO · LONDON · SYDNEY · AUCKLAND

RL: 6, AGES 012 AND UP

DANNY

A Bantam Book / May 2000

Cover photography by Michael Segal.

Produced by 17th Street Productions,
an Alloy Online, Inc. company.
33 West 17th Street
New York, NY 10011.

ISBN: 0-553-49322-1

Visit us on the Web! www.randomhouse.com/teens

Published simultaneously in the United States and Canada

Bantam Books is an imprint of Random House Children's Books, a
division of Random House, Inc. BANTAM BOOKS and the rooster
colophon are registered trademarks of Random House, Inc. Bantam Books,
1540 Broadway, New York, New York 10036.

PRINTED IN THE UNITED STATES OF AMERICA

OPM   0 9 8 7 6 5 4 3 2 1

One

"LET SUMMER BEGIN!" Kevin Ford declared as he hurled his backpack across the living room. It hit the torn couch against the wall with a poof of dust, then landed on the old carpet with a thud.

"Guess it's the cleaning lady's year off," Johnny Ford commented, waving dust motes from the air in front of his face.

"Cleanliness is for the weak," Kevin scoffed.

Danny Ford rolled his eyes. It was hard to believe: Two days ago he was in a classroom at Spring Valley High. Now he was at the beach.

This is it, he thought, surveying the apartment and letting his duffel bag hit the floor. *This is where I'm going to spend the summer. The wet, wild . . . widiculous summer before my junior year. Shouldn't I be just a little more psyched?*

It was a bittersweet deal, he figured. Sweet in

1

that his parents were letting him and his brothers spend their summer in Surf City, one of the hottest beach towns on the southern California coast. Bitter in that he had to live *with* his two brothers in a rattrap apartment. Wasn't it bad enough that he spent his whole life sandwiched between seventeen-year-old Johnny and fifteen-year-old Kevin like some sixteen-year-old cold cut? And now he had to share his space with them during his summer vacation.

Ha, he thought, *this ain't no va-cay. I'll be working at the restaurant every day just to break even on this little money pit.*

Pit was a generous term. The door of the apartment opened into a small, dank living room with a couch, a lounge chair, and a coffee table that looked ready to collapse under the weight of a soda bottle. To the left was the kitchen, a space marked off by stained, peeling linoleum and another precarious table. The stove had two gas burners and probably couldn't reheat a pizza. The refrigerator was small, squat, and rattled and hummed louder than U2.

The whole place was done up in an early seventies paneling the color of stale caramel. The meager decorations consisted of a painting of an old man in a dinghy and three crookedly hung sand dollars, each mounted and framed on red felt.

"Cool, cozy, comfortable," Kevin declared. He jumped over the duct-taped arm of the Barcalounger that was so rat eaten, it made the chair in Frasier Crane's living room look positively chic. In midair Kevin crossed his feet and assumed a relaxation position. The springs squealed on impact, sending up a mushroom cloud of mildew as thick as a feather pillow. "Ahhh . . . I do believe I can live here."

"You could live in a hollowed-out pumpkin," Johnny said, rubbing the dust out of his brown eyes.

"Nah, too humid," Kevin replied as he looked through his framed fingers at a space in the corner—no doubt plotting where the TV should go. "But give me a shoe box, a burlap sack, and some blank paper, and I'm good to go."

"Artists have to suffer, Kev," Danny said. He stretched muscles, cramped from the four-hour Jeep ride. "You're too enthusiastic."

"Suffering's in the eye of the sufferer," Kevin stated, now framing the front window. He leaned forward, gazing more intently at the world through the glass. "Hey . . . not a bad view. You can see the water."

Johnny dumped his bag on the kitchen table a few feet away. Somehow it didn't collapse. "That's why we're paying for 'ocean view,' brainiac. You get this close to the boardwalk, they can charge you seven bills a week for a wet shoe box." He ran his hand along the kitchen countertop, scowled, and quickly wiped his fingers on his shorts. "Man, it smells like Dad's bowling-ball bag in here."

Danny smirked. His brother wasn't that far off. In one breath you could smell the clean salt air, the

3

french fries off the boardwalk, and coconut suntan oil (hopefully smeared on tan female limbs). In the next breath you got old sweat dried into couch cushions and leftover lobster.

"I'm just glad we found a place," Danny pointed out. "We were lucky. We waited way too long."

"Hey, you were the one who wasn't sure if he wanted to come," Kevin shot back. He yanked the handle on the side of the lounge chair and reclined it with a loud creak and thud. "Are you ever sure of anything, Danny?"

"Gee, I'm not sure," Danny replied, though he felt his face growing red. The truth really did hurt sometimes. Danny truly wasn't sure about a lot of things.

He felt pressure mounting from all sides. He was sixteen. He had to start "getting serious" . . . "thinking about the future" . . . "deciding what he wanted to do with his life." Name your cliché, he heard them all—and from all directions. Parents. Teachers. Friends. And older brother, of course.

Johnny was the example everyone used. He worked hard. He had been accepted at a great college. And he'd probably go on to make lots of money and make everyone proud. Which was great for Johnny. There was just one problem. Since Johnny was doing it, everyone naturally expected Danny to do the same thing.

But he didn't know what he wanted.

Nope, not a clue.

He hoped that this summer would show him

something. Anything. Actually, he knew that was asking too much. But his life was such a gray area. His brothers knew exactly what they wanted to do with their lives. Johnny was a numbers whiz. He loved money. Well, everyone loved money, but Johnny truly *loved* it. He knew how to make it and, better yet, how to keep it. He was all set to attend Allman College in the fall for, you guessed it, finance.

Kevin, on the other hand, was a one-eighty spin. At fifteen he could draw, and that was about it. But, man, *what* he could draw with pen, pencil, charcoal, and occasionally paint. Anything and everything, as long as it fit his strange worldview. And if it didn't fit? Kevin made it fit. And he was great at it. He could create whole comic strips or serious portraits—yet his signature style always shone through. Danny figured if Kevin could use his titanic charm to get the Kate Winslets of the world to take off their robes and pose for him, he had a pretty bright future. Might even make some money.

There's that word again, Danny thought. Money. *The word that brought on all those other words:* future, college, career, direction.

Danny knew what those words meant, but they didn't apply to him. At least not yet.

What did he like, after all? He'd rolled it through his head countless times. The likes-dislikes. The pros-cons. The possibilities that seemed oh so impossible.

Music. That was it. He liked music. But he

couldn't play it. He'd tried both the guitar and piano and lasted maybe two weeks on both. Playing music had to be in the soul. You were supposed to feel something magical when you picked up an instrument. Danny felt nothing.

But when he listened to music? Danny was moved. His heart raced, his spine tingled. He felt alive. It didn't matter what kind of music: metal, punk, ska, hip-hop, and good old rock and roll. He loved the purer forms as well: blues, jazz, and classical.

His CD collection was in the triple digits. He'd have bought more if he had the money (that word again), but he also maintained an extensive bootleg collection that he taped from friends and the public library. All those cost him were a few bucks' worth of blank cassettes.

But what good did it do him? To enter the musical realm in college, you had to play. You couldn't major in "listening." And even if you could, what kind of a job could you get?

DJ.

Great, Danny thought. *I'll play weddings and bar mitzvahs for the rest of my life, one step below Adam Sandler because at least he could* sing. *What would that make me? The Wedding Jockey?*

Danny's day-mare was broken by Johnny clapping. "Okay, bros, let's get the Jeep unpacked and set this joint up. We can draw straws on who gets the couch."

Danny and Kevin just stared at their older brother.

Johnny clapped again. "Come on, bums, stop acting homeless, and let's get to work. We have a lot to do, and tomorrow's no holiday."

Kevin turned to Danny with a quizzical look. "Who invited Dad?"

"Not me," Danny replied, not budging.

"Don't start this again," Johnny grumbled, folding his arms across his chest. "Mom and Dad never would have let you two come if I wasn't here to watch over you." He shook his head. "Besides, you think all our stuff is just going to walk itself up here? Someone has to kick your butts, or nothing would ever get done."

"Another Dad-ism," Kevin muttered, wearily rising from the lounge chair. "You really need some new material, John Boy."

Johnny shrugged. "Fine. I'm hauling my stuff up here, and I'm taking the back bedroom."

"You are not," Kevin growled. "We draw straws, just like you said."

"Hey, bud, you snooze, you lose on the sleeping quarters," Johnny told him. "I'm not playing nursemaid to you guys. Your gear can sit in the parking lot all summer for all I care. But it is *not* sitting in my Jeep. Get it?"

Kevin glowered. "Yeah, you never know when Mr. Happy here might get a visit from the Ice Princess."

Danny smiled. "Hope the Jeep has fresh antifreeze, John Boy."

Johnny's face darkened, and Danny immediately

saw the old familiar "madman" Johnny face. He knew his brothers' facial tics like veteran actors in a long-running TV show. The "madman" showed up anytime anyone criticized Johnny's girlfriend of three years, Jane.

"I'm not biting, Kevin," Johnny said coolly. "The ride was too long, and the summer's just starting. You just have to deal with the fact that Jane's gonna be around. I love her, and that's the way it is."

"Awwww," Kevin cooed. "How sweet. Have some insulin with that sugar?"

Johnny's face hardened, and he took a step toward Kevin. Danny moved between them, bumping chests with his older brother. "I think what my younger brother, Kevin, is trying to say is that Jane is perfectly welcome here anytime, Johnny. But just because you have a steady girl doesn't mean you get automatic dibs on a bedroom."

"Says who?" Johnny challenged.

"Says the unsilent majority, pal," Kevin shot back. "Two bedrooms. Three guys. We draw straws just like we agreed three months ago."

"Hold it, hold it, hold it." Danny held up his hands. His brothers glared at him as if he had changed the channel in the middle of the Super Bowl. "This is ridiculous. It's the first day. I'm sick of you guys already. I'll take the couch for the first month of the summer. Okay? Then I get a bedroom, and you two can fight over the last two months. Does that work for you knuckleheads?"

They chewed on it for a moment. Finally Kevin spoke. "We should draw straws."

"Forget the straws," Johnny replied, turning toward the door. "Danny, if you want the couch, great, man. I don't care. Whatever the two of you decide is fine by me. I'm not wasting my time on this kiddie turf war anymore. All I know is that two months out of three, I get a bed."

"Just like we all do, Johnny," Danny replied.

Johnny nodded, kicked open the apartment door, and disappeared.

Kevin sidled up to Danny, smiling. "Nice to have him along, don't you think?"

"What did you expect?" Danny asked.

Kevin clapped a hand on Danny's shoulder and mock hugged his brother. "You know what I expect, Dan-o? I'll tell you what I expect. I expect nothing less than the summer of my life. I expect to meet and fall in love with four to five beautiful older women per month. I expect to eat leftover pizza and have garlic breath. I expect to fill countless sketch pads with the bikini-clad forms of nubile beach beauties. I expect parties, romance, and endless intrigue—you know, as seen on TV. But most of all, and I think you'll agree with me on this one, I expect to bring home a big, fat volleyball trophy and a check for ten thousand dollars."

Danny smiled at his younger brother.

"Yeah," Danny replied, punching Kevin's fist with his own. "That sounds about right."

★   ★   ★

The Surf City 3-on-3 Beach Volleyball Tournament was the Ford brothers' primary reason for existing. *If we don't kill each other first,* Danny thought.

As Johnny and Kevin carted their stuff up the three flights of steps from the Jeep, Danny unpacked his gear in the living room (as much as he dared unpack clothing in that "public" space. Who needed his boxers paraded in front of guests?). He hadn't packed much: one duffel bag, a CD boom box, a CD Walkman, a cassette Walkman, and a large plastic crate full of CDs and tapes. Danny had brought roughly one-third of his collection because of space. This had meant boiling down his music stash into the bare essentials: greatest-hits collections and live albums, which gave him the most music in the least amount of space. There were some classics that he couldn't live without, of course, but the three days it took him to pack his music was an endless torture of indecision and sacrifice.

Let's not talk about indecision anymore, Danny told himself. Living in a constant gray area was bad enough. He didn't need to torture himself with it.

He forced himself to think about something important. Something that raised the stakes and got his adrenaline pumping: volleyball.

Johnny was the one who had suggested it. Danny remembered the day six months ago when his older bro assembled them at the local burger joint and presented them with a daring idea. "Dudes, listen up. You remember how we always talked about playing v-ball for something meaning-ful? Well, listen to this. . . ."

Johnny had gone on to describe the mother of all beach-volleyball tournaments: the Surf City War. The official name was the Fizz Cola Surf City 3-on-3 Beach Volleyball Tournament, but v-ballers up and down the California coast referred to it sim-ply as The War. Anyone who ever spiked one into another guy's face knew the significance of this tournament. If you won, you took home a five-foot trophy, a lifetime supply of Fizz Cola, and ten thou-sand dollars in cash.

But that was just the hardware.

What you really won was the undisputed bragging rights to the most coveted amateur-beach-volleyball championship on the West Coast. Danny liked to put it this way: Pretend the World Series is a kaiser roll. Slice it in half, pile on some Stanley Cup mustard, a few slices of Olympic gold medal, and a generous helping of Super Bowl, and that sweet-tasting sand-wich would be eaten in one sitting by the Surf City War trophy.

"Heads up!" Johnny screamed.

Danny heard the familiar slap of skin on ball be-fore the cry and instinctively turned, hands up. He caught the volleyball on the fly.

"You're gonna have to do better than that, bro." Danny laughed. "Your serve needs work."

"So, show me the mustard, hot dog," Johnny jeered, gesturing for Danny to bring it on.

Danny did.

He tossed the ball lightly and popped it with his palm, cutting across the axis with his fingers. The ball sprang from his hand, firing toward Johnny like a comet. But halfway there, it began to fade away from him toward the kitchen. By the time the ball reached Johnny, it had curled a good two feet to the right, losing none of its velocity.

Johnny lunged for it but missed. The ball caromed off the kitchen cabinets and floor like a wayward bullet.

"Ace, dude," Danny declared. "You lose."

Johnny snagged the ball and palmed it. "I still don't know how you do that, Danny. You serve like that in the tournament, and we're golden."

Danny shrugged. "The tourney's two months away. We'll go crazy between now and then."

"No way," Johnny replied. "Between practice and pickup games on the beach, we'll be sharper than ever. I guarantee it."

"You're George Foreman now?" Kevin asked, emerging from his bedroom. "You could use a muffler."

Johnny tossed him the ball. "Just getting psyched. I can taste that ten-grand check already."

"Forget the money, man," Kevin replied, dribbling the ball through his legs. "I'll be the youngest v-ball champ on the West Coast. I'll be Velcro, and chicks'll be felt."

"Pun intended, right?" Johnny said with a smirk.

"Of course," Kevin replied, wiggling his eyebrows.

Danny was grateful for the moment of peace. They were rare. Volleyball was the glue that held the Ford brothers together. If that fell apart, they would probably kill each other. They were so different. The championship was a prime example. Johnny wanted the cash. Kevin wanted the fame. What did that leave for Danny? The lifetime supply of Fizz Cola.

Not bloody likely.

No, Danny clung to volleyball because it gave his life direction. When the money talk, the college chat, or the future fantasies got too intense, there was music. And there was volleyball. In a way, the Surf City championship was the ultimate goal for him. But on the other hand, winning it scared him. Not because he was intimidated by the competition or afraid of failure.

He was scared of winning because after that there would be nothing in his life left for him to shoot for.

Soon the day grew long, and the sun set over the water outside their front window. It was then that the Ford brothers took advantage of the one civilized perk of their rattrap apartment: the balcony. It was tiny, no more than three feet by ten feet, but it was still a balcony that faced the ocean.

Danny took a deep breath of salt air and sighed. Not bad. He could see the whitecaps now turning crimson in the glare. The waves crashed, devouring the dusk surfers like predinner snacks. On the sand the last of the shriveled sun worshipers folded their chairs for the night.

And three stories below the brothers, rolling off in either direction like a spool of toy railroad, was the Surf City boardwalk. The flashing lights were just winking on. The pizza and fries hit the counters and filled the air with the thick scent of grease. People trundled along, moms wheeling their jogger strollers, tourists slurping down ice cream cones, kids tugging the parents' arms for more, more, more. In-line skaters click-clacked along, weaving in and out of all of them.

"I love the beach," Kevin said wistfully, watching a gorgeous redhead in a black bikini top and cutoff shorts skate her way toward Mexico.

"Yeah, well, we'll see how much you like it after a couple of weeks of cleaning up after the snobby slobs at the hotel, Kev," Danny replied, leaning on the rail and sipping a soda.

Kevin shrugged, as if his job as a cabana boy at the ritzy Surf City Resort Hotel was no sweat off his back. "At least I won't be schlepping buffalo wings for ten-percent tips at Jabba's Palace."

Danny chuckled. Because that's exactly what he was going to be doing. Jabba's Palace was a greasy spoon disguised as fine dining about twenty blocks down the boardwalk. It was named after its owner, an overfed monster of a man who was known only as Jabba. Danny had met him just once, when the brothers came to Surf City in the spring to secure summer jobs. But Jabba wasn't the kind of man you forgot.

"Remember, guys," Johnny cautioned. "It's not about the jobs. It's about the money. We have to pay for this palace."

"That's easy for you to say," Danny replied. "You're a lifeguard at the poshest hotel in town. You get to do the *Baywatch* thing in front of rich, lonely women in bathing suits."

Johnny was set to work the Surf City Resort Hotel's private beach and pool, a cushy summer job if there ever was one.

"Hey, all you had to do was get certified," Johnny shot back. "I put in a lot of hours for that. It's no picnic."

Kevin grinned. "All I have to say is that if I hear, 'Oh, cabana boy, get me a towel,' from your mouth just one time, you're toast. Got me?"

Johnny laughed, shoving his smaller but wiry little brother. "Okay, shrimp. Do your worst."

Kevin held up his hands in surrender. "Just getting it out in the open right now. Just because we work at the same place doesn't mean you can boss me around."

"Whatever you say, Kev," Johnny snapped sarcastically. "Whatever you say."

"If you guys are through barking at each other," Danny interrupted, "I'd like to propose a toast." He raised his plastic twenty ouncer of Fizz Cola. "To The War. Here's hoping we survive each other long enough to win it."

His brothers nodded and raised their own sodas. "To The War," they said in unison.

They drank. And for a moment Danny felt like he truly belonged to something special, something beyond even brotherhood. They were united in a single purpose—something that was bigger than anything they'd ever done by themselves. They needed each other like never before.

Danny enjoyed the feeling. But it was going to be a long, hot summer. And none of them really knew what would happen. Still, Danny savored the moment and the first sunset in their new home.

Because for that moment the possibilities really were endless.

TWO

"**G**IMME A CHEESY fish, a side of waffle fries, and three blue heart attacks!" bellowed Archie, a hippie wanna-be with a long, red ponytail and grease stains on his apron.

Danny tried to do the translation in his head: *Cheesy fish . . . That's a tuna melt. . . . Waffle fries are, well, waffle fries . . . and three blue heart attacks are three half-pound burgers stuffed with blue-cheese dressing.* There were also gold (cheddar) heart attacks, red (chili) heart attacks, Italian (alfredo sauce) heart attacks, and, believe it or not, canine (hot-dog) heart attacks. Leave it to Jabba to stuff a hamburger with a hot dog.

If all of that was too much, you could order from Jabba's "light" menu: Caesar salad with anchovies.

"I *do* cook light," Danny had overheard Jabba say earlier to a customer. "I use butter instead of lard!"

Jabba's Palace was basically a hole-in-the-wall.

But on the Surf City boardwalk, that didn't matter. Several sets of peeling shutter doors opened onto the boards, providing some relief from the heavy air. Ceiling fans spun overhead, the blades coated with greasy dust. The tables were ancient, made of thick wood and covered with paper tablecloths that were crumpled up and tossed in the garbage when each feeding frenzy was through.

At lunch and dinner people lined up out the door, waiting for a table. Grease was popular, after all, and Jabba's heart attacks were renowned up and down the boards. If you came to Surf City, you ate at Jabba's. It was that simple.

Jabba roamed his restaurant like a tank, cracking jokes and cracking cholesterol records. He didn't really resemble the *Star Wars* Jabba, but he was in a physical league of his own. He stood about five-seven and had to weigh at least four hundred pounds. His whole body was involved with each step. The lower half of his face was covered with black-gray hair, which made his crew cut even more strange. His cackle could be heard out on the boardwalk. And his jokes were terrible.

Danny just tried to keep his head down and his orders straight. The wait staff had a language all its own, and he found himself having to learn on the fly. Burgers were heart attacks (because Jabba marinated the meat in a garlic butter sauce before grilling), hot dogs were canines, buffalo wings were lipstick, and nachos were junk piles because of the size of the servings.

He sidled up to table six. The couple there ordered two heart attacks, blue and gold, a dozen lipsticks, and fries. Easy one.

Table four was a family of five. Three heart attacks, a cheesy fish, and four canines. Fries and Fizz all around.

Danny posted his orders as fast as he could. Jabba liked turnover, turnover, turnover.

Table seven, seven attacks and seven pitchers of beer. "Seven pitchers?" Danny asked, glancing up from his notepad.

The table was filled with little old ladies in sun hats.

"Seven pitchers, kid," one old lady grumbled in a voice that sounded like a dirt road. "You heard right."

Danny grinned. "No problem."

The day rolled on like that. He was scheduled to work from noon to ten, with one half-hour break for dinner. At minimum wage plus tips Danny figured to break even after rent and living expenses. *Ha,* he thought. *You have to have a life to have living expenses.* His one day off a week, Monday, left him with minimal free time.

I didn't want a tan anyway, he reasoned.

"Yo, kid, where's my burger?" barked a customer to his left.

Uh-oh. "You ordered a tuna melt, sir."

The guy, an overweight father of two, rolled his eyes and glared at his family as if to say: What kind of moron am I dealing with? "No, kid," he replied with mock patience. "I ordered a hot-dog burger ten minutes ago. The rest of my family has their food. I got squat. You wanna check your little notebook again?"

Danny frantically flipped pages. His face grew hot.

The guy cursed. "Can you believe this? Yo, kid. Forget the notebook. Just bring me my burger."

"Hot-dog burger?" Danny confirmed. "Not a tuna melt?"

The guy balled up a napkin in his fist and forced a smile. "Very good, kid. There may be a future for you in food service yet."

"What's the problem here?" came a loud voice.

Danny felt Jabba's presence before the man spoke. *Like a disturbance in the Force,* he thought glumly. *Great. Now I'm in for it.*

"Your boy here," the guy growled, gesturing at Danny with contempt, "is trying to cover his butt. I'm waitin' on a hot-dog burger for half an hour now."

"Half an hour?" Danny blurted out. "More like ten minutes!"

Jabba turned full bore on Danny. "I don't know how they wait tables in Pleasantville or wherever you came from, kid, but here in the big leagues we don't usually refer to our customers as liars."

Rage churned in Danny's belly. The guy at the table smirked in triumph. Jabba folded his arms across his thick chest, breathing through his mouth like an idling freight train. "Well?" he asked impatiently.

Danny took a deep breath and swallowed his anger. "I'll get the burger."

Jabba grabbed his sleeve. "Hold it, kid. Don't you have something else to say to these nice people?"

Boy, do I, Danny thought. He glared at the guy and his smug little family and tried not to lose it. "I'm sorry, sir. I'll bring your burger right out."

"Hurry it up, will you?" the guy replied. "My kids want to hit the Spiral Terror before the line gets too long."

The Spiral Terror. The killer roller coaster on the amusement pier. *Hope they lose their lunches,* Danny thought. "Right away, sir," he said snappily, and headed for the kitchen. As he moved away, he clearly heard Jabba's comment to the man:

"That's what you get for minimum wage these days. . . ."

Danny was allowed to take his break at four-thirty, before the hard-core dinner rush. Jabba allowed his employees to have a free soda and frics. Anything else had to be paid for.

Danny had to get out of there. In four and a half hours he'd served something like fifty heart attacks, which he figured was illegal in some states. He needed air and space and sunlight. Danny poured himself a tall Fizz and snagged some waffle fries in a plastic basket lined with wax paper. He drowned them in ketchup to cover the grease and slipped between two tables and out a door to the boardwalk.

He took a deep breath and sighed, picturing thick wafts of steam floating out of his clothes. Jabba's Palace was like a chamber of bad breath. Danny hadn't realized just how bad it was until he smelled the clean salt air.

Finally, he thought. *Peace . . .*

He took a step toward a bench on the other side of the boardwalk.

Then someone slammed into him at what felt like sixty miles an hour. The air whooshed out of Danny's lungs. The boardwalk felt like concrete on his shoulder and hip. And the french fries, soda, and ketchup felt like a hot blanket of slime on his face.

Aw, man . . .

"Dude!" screamed a deep, enraged voice. "Scumbag! Moron! Dog! Get up!"

Danny stared up into the face of a freak. His head was shaved clean on the sides, leaving a bristly blue patch up on top. His eyes were wide and angry. His front teeth were crooked, and his eye-teeth were long and vampiric. A shark-tooth earring dangled from one ear. He wore a torn Marilyn Manson T-shirt and canvas shorts low on his waist. The shirt was stained with ketchup. His arms were flexed and ready. Veins ran up his forearms like thick phone wiring.

"I said get up!" he repeated.

Danny slowly rose, trying hard to figure out what had just happened. Then he saw the upside-down skateboard stained with ketchup. This guy had been motoring down the boardwalk and slammed into him. Danny's dinner was spread out in a ten-foot radius. And this guy now wanted a piece of him.

Danny straightened up to his full height. The skateboarder was still a good three inches taller. His teeth looked even worse close up.

"Why you in my way, pretty boy?" the guy demanded, his face closing in on Danny's. "You got ketchup all over my shirt! I *hate* ketchup!"

"Smear him, Doberman," came another male voice.

Three more skate rats skidded to a halt around the pair. All of them were dressed in various versions of Doberman, though they were smaller and skinnier. One rat hauled a boom box cranked up to distortion.

Finally a fourth skate rat clattered up. A girl. She stomped on the fin of her board, popping it vertical and grabbing it in midair. She had pink streaks running through her shoulder-length brown hair. Her ears were loaded down with rings of varying shapes and sizes. Her shredded jeans revealed flashes of smooth leg underneath. She wore a black spaghetti-string tank top that hugged her form like a second skin.

It was a real nice form, Danny thought.

But what drew Danny's stare was the girl's eyes. Smoky gray eyes, wide and clear. Full of casual amusement at Danny.

"Hey, cupcake," Doberman grunted, smacking Danny's shoulder. "I'm talkin' to you."

Danny broke away from the girl. "So? What's the problem? You weren't looking where you were going."

Doberman's eyes widened. "Me? *Me?* Moron boy, you are about three seconds away from instant death."

Danny smiled and wiped his face with a crumpled napkin. "If it takes three seconds, it's not very instant, is it?"

The skate rats surrounding them ooohed as if Danny had just smacked Doberman in the face with a white glove. And maybe he had.

Danny had never considered himself a fighter. But he wasn't one to back down either. Right now he was tired, frustrated, and still facing more than five hours of work. All he wanted to do was have a soda and fries. But surveying the overturned basket and crushed soda cup, he knew that wasn't happening.

Doberman grinned his nasty teeth and flexed. "Okay, pretty boy. Prepare to eat your tongue."

"Dobie, don't," the girl interrupted.

Doberman scowled but didn't take his eyes off Danny. "Shut up, Raven. You know I hate ketchup."

Raven laughed sarcastically. "What I know is you're acting like a jerk again. This guy didn't mean it. Leave him alone."

The frustration grew in Doberman. Whatever hold this Raven had on him—call it a leash for Doberman—was working. Danny hoped so anyway.

There was no way he could take this guy . . . and he couldn't back down now.

"Okay, pretty boy," Doberman said, massaging a fist, his restraint obvious. "I have a better idea. We'll play a little game. If you win, you walk. If you lose, you go down. *Comprende?*"

Danny shook his head and looked back at Jabba's Palace. "I don't have time for this—"

Doberman yanked Danny back by the shirt. "Make time, pretty boy."

Rage overflowed in Danny. He batted Doberman's hand away and got in his face. "Okay, pal, what's it gonna be?"

Doberman yanked the boom box from his bud and brandished it like a weapon. "Simple game, pretty boy." He put his ear to the thudding speaker. "You hear that?"

Danny shrugged. "The whole block can hear it. So what?"

"So, pretty boy . . ." Doberman grinned devilishly. "Name that tune."

Danny glanced at the boom box. The speakers were shot. The sound getting through barely resembled music at all.

One of the skate rats giggled. "He's toast, dude."

Danny surveyed the circle surrounding him. They all looked the same: badly dyed and shaved hair, torn concert shirts, ripped jeans slung low. Their eyes were playful and indignant. They seemed smug in the knowledge that there was no chance

25

Danny could possibly recognize this little musical slice of their rebellious life. No chance at all.

The girl, Raven, smirked the worst of them all. She rocked back and forth on her heels to the beat, fingering a skull ring on her left hand. Her smoky gray eyes regarded Danny with pure amusement—and a hint of boredom. As if she enjoyed his challenge of Doberman but knew that it would all be over in a few seconds.

They all figured Danny was played.

That's when he blurted out, "'Chainsaw Perfume,' by the Dustmites."

Doberman blinked. "Say what?"

Danny smiled. "You heard me."

"Wrong, pretty boy." Doberman shook his head. "Not even close. It's 'CIA Is for Apple,' by Ball Peen Hammer." He flexed his forearms. "You lose. Prepare to die."

"Dobie—," one of the rats began.

"Shut up, Skunk," Doberman growled.

"He's *right,* Dobe," another rat argued.

Doberman whirled on the guy named Skunk. "He is *not* right, dude. That's Ball Peen Hammer. I gave you the tape myself."

"Yeah." Skunk nodded. "And I switched it a half hour ago to the Dustmites. I was sick of the noise."

"He's right, Dobe," the other rat repeated.

Doberman was really frustrated now. "So what if he's right? He got ketchup all over me."

Doberman balled a fist . . .

26

Here we go, Danny thought.

He prepared to dodge it, but before anything could happen, the punk girl stepped between him and Doberman. In the process she brushed against Danny. He could smell her hair, a combination of fragrant shampoo and mousse. She had a small mole on the back of her neck.

"Fair's fair, Dobie," she said to the big guy, gently pushing him away. "He knew the song. You didn't even know the band."

Doberman bristled. "I don't care about right or wrong. Pretty boy was *in my way.*"

Raven smirked. "Everyone's in your way. That's why you're Doberman." Then she turned and stared right into Danny's eyes. "But maybe pretty boy's a cooler cat than anyone thinks."

Danny gulped. This girl had enough ear piercings to hang laundry, and her hair was a rainbow of fruit flavors. But she was gorgeous beyond the hardware. He could see her face so much better close-up. Some black eyeliner around those smoky grays. A beautiful smile. He couldn't help the butterflies in his belly. They fluttered even worse when she stared at him . . . like she was doing right now. He didn't say a word.

"Let's roll, dude," Skunk suggested. "This scene's played out."

"I agree," Raven replied, still staring at Danny. "Don't you agree, Doberman?"

Doberman kicked over his skateboard and stepped on it. "Yeah. Right. Whatever. Fine."

27

Raven smiled at him. "Thought so."

Doberman leveled a deadly stare at Danny. "Watch yourself, pretty boy. Next time there won't be any games. Next time it's just me and you and the black 'n' blue. *Comprende?*"

Danny shrugged. "Sure, why not?"

Doberman pushed off and rolled down the boardwalk. Skunk and the other two guys followed suit. But Raven didn't move from her spot next to Danny. She was only inches away.

"Thanks for holding him off," Danny said, trying to catch her gray eyes again. But she was gazing down the boards after her friends.

"De nada," she replied.

Danny didn't say anything right away. Neither did Raven. She didn't budge either.

What's her deal? he wondered. Not that he minded her staying . . .

Finally she turned and met his gaze. "So . . . just how cool a cat are you?"

Danny smiled. "How cool can anyone be when they're covered with ketchup?"

Raven laughed.

"Yo, Raven!" Doberman called from down the boardwalk. "Let's roll!"

Raven dropped her board and stepped onto it. Her eyes never left Danny's.

She's leaving, he thought. *Say something. Say anything. Pull a John Cusack.* But nothing came to mind. All Danny could do was watch her push off and slowly roll away.

She smirked and gave a mocking buh-bye wave. "Later, pretty boy," she said. "If you're lucky."

All Danny could do was stand there, struck dumb. In seconds Raven pushed off for real and disappeared into the crowd. She was gone.

Danny blinked stupidly, smelling like Fizz and fries.

Who *was* that girl?

What I Look for in a Guy

by Raven

1. Attitude. 'Nuf said.

2. Skating ability. I mean, a guy's gotta be able to keep up with me.

3. A sense of humor. It's a cliché, but hey, it's a cliché for a reason, right? Being able to laugh with someone is the best.

4. Intelligence. He doesn't have to be a brain, but I need someone to make me think.

5. Piercings. (Okay, I can overlook this.)

6. Eyes. I don't know—something about the eyes always grabs me. They're honest, I guess.

Three

THE NEXT MORNING Danny, Johnny, and Kevin hit the beach for a quick hour of volleyball practice. They found a deserted beach court several blocks away—not many people played beach volleyball at nine in the morning. They warmed up by casually knocking the ball around. Johnny and Kevin stood on one side, setting and spiking. Danny took the other side, serving.

"I think I'm going to have the smell of towel detergent on me permanently," Kevin complained, referring to his first day on the job. "Do you know how many towels I delivered yesterday? In one day? Guess."

"I'm not going to guess," Johnny replied, making a V with his arms and expertly setting up the ball so Kevin could spike it. "Besides, no matter how rotten your day was, it couldn't beat mine. My new lifeguard partner is Kylie Smith."

31

"And that's supposed to mean something?" Danny asked.

"Guess!" Kevin demanded, simultaneously slamming the ball over the net and into the sand.

"Dude, just guess," Danny grumbled, fetching the ball.

"One hundred eighty-two," Kevin declared, clapping sand off his hands. "That's one-eight-two. In one day. I didn't know there were that many wet rich people in the world."

Danny tossed up the ball and slapped it across the net, a straight serve with no English. "You make any tips, cabana boy?"

"Yeah," Kevin scoffed, shaking his head. He took a step back, lined up Danny's serve, and popped it straight up for Johnny. "Ten bucks and one practice-safe-sex tip from old Mr. Moran. That guy's like two hundred years old, and he needs five towels to dry off after being in the pool. What a gig."

Johnny timed Kevin's set perfectly, leaving the ground and stretching his body to its full length. His muscles worked in poetic unison as he walloped the volleyball across the net and into the sand at the speed of sound. That was Johnny's strength—his height and form allowed him to generate incredible spikes.

"Kylie Smith is Jane's total enemy. Can you believe that? We come all the way to Surf City, and I end up working with someone that not only does my girlfriend know, she hates." Johnny sighed.

"But, hey. I'll deal. The cash is great, and that's what I'm in it for." He turned to Danny. "How about you? Make any money?"

That word again. Danny chuckled. "Yeah, lots. Ten hours. Twenty-two in tips. And a faceful of ketchup."

"What do you mean?" Kevin asked, laughing.

Danny told them about his close encounter with Doberman and friends. He included the fries, ketchup, and music test. But he didn't mention Raven.

Kevin laughed even harder. "Cool, Dan-o. Very smooth."

Johnny scooped up the volleyball from the sand and eyed his younger bro skeptically. "You faced this skinhead down all by yourself?"

Danny shrugged. "I wouldn't call him a skinhead. He was just a skate rat. But yeah, I faced him down. All by myself." Then he thought of Raven. "Basically."

"Aha," Johnny said, nodding as he tossed the ball from hand to hand. "What's basically?"

Danny felt himself blushing. Luckily he was on the other side of the net, where they couldn't see.

"Speak up, Dan-o," Kevin called, folding his arms across his chest. "I didn't hear you."

Danny shrugged. "Well . . . I sort of met a chick."

Johnny and Kevin shared a look and burst out laughing. "You *sort* of met a chick?" Johnny asked. "How do you *sort* of meet a chick?"

"We weren't formally introduced," Danny replied with forced impatience, as if he didn't want to talk about Raven, even though he really did. "I caught her name when the rats talked to her."

"What, she was walking down the boardwalk?" Kevin inquired.

Danny shook his head. "She was with them. She stepped between me and Doberman just before the first swing."

Johnny looked quizzically at Danny, then casually bumped the ball over the net at him. "The chick's a skate rat?"

"Basically," Danny replied again. He caught the volleyball and held it, grateful to have something to do with his hands. "She doesn't look like a rat, though."

"She hot?" Kevin asked expectantly.

Danny nodded, thinking of Raven's gray eyes. "Smokin'."

"Of course she is," Johnny said. "Except for the shaved head, right?"

"You wish," Danny shot back. "The girl's totally hot. Why's that so hard to believe?"

Johnny shrugged. "I've never seen a hot skate rat."

"Oh, I get it," Danny replied. "If a girl isn't fit for the J. Crew catalog, she couldn't possibly be hot. Is that it?"

Johnny moved forward to the net, spidering his fingers through it and letting his weight pull it down slightly. He hung there. "Are you dating this girl, Danny?"

"Nope," Danny replied, coolly twirling the volleyball on his finger.

Kevin laughed. "Then why are you so sensitive about her?"

The ball spun on Danny's finger for two seconds and fell to the sand. "The girl helped me out. I said she happened to be hot. You guys seem to disagree even though you weren't there and didn't see her. You assume since she owns a skateboard that she must have pepperoni pizza for a face."

"I think he likes her, Kev," Johnny announced.

"I think you're right, John Boy," Kevin agreed.

Danny bristled, pressing his hands into the volleyball—hard. "So what if I do?"

Johnny's grin was a challenge. "Does she have a shaved head?"

"Nope."

"Dyed hair?"

Danny paused. "Yep."

"Green?"

"Streaks of pink."

"How nice. Multiple body piercings?"

"Yep."

Johnny's grin widened. "A tattoo?"

"I didn't see one."

"Ah." Johnny sighed dramatically. "Well . . . she's a real departure from your usual dating specimens, bro."

Danny knew Johnny was right, but he wasn't going to let him know that he knew. Letting Johnny win an argument was like letting Saddam

Hussein win the Gulf War. "What do you mean?"

Johnny let go of the volleyball net and ducked underneath to Danny's side. "Let's take a nice sample group. Say, the last three girls you dated. Who were they?" Johnny tapped his chin, remembering. "Oh yeah. Julie Horn . . . Carol Smith . . . and who was the other girl . . ."

"Kathy Hughes," Kevin added.

"That's the one," Johnny agreed.

Danny tucked the ball under his arm, trying to stay calm. "What's your point?"

"All those girls are really cute, and really nice, and really *normal*," Johnny said, rattling off their traits on his fingers with a special emphasis on the last one. "I'm just saying that I'm surprised you'd find a skate rat attractive, that's all. Don't be so defensive."

Danny shrugged. "I find hot chicks hot. She could be an alien. I'd still think she's hot."

"That alien chick on *Roswell* is pretty hot," Kevin offered.

Johnny chuckled. "All I'm saying is that it's our third day here. There are ten thousand sorority babes in bikinis concentrated in a thirty-block radius. And you want to date Wednesday Addams."

Danny tossed the ball at Johnny, maybe harder than he intended. Maybe not. "You're forgetting one thing, dude."

Johnny caught the ball with a smack. He smiled at the force of the throw. "What's that?"

"Wednesday Addams grew up to be Christina Ricci."

Kevin burst out laughing and high-fived Danny. "The man has a point, Johnny. Maybe we should meet this girl."

Danny grinned himself. "That might prove difficult."

"Why?" Kevin asked.

"Because," Danny said with a sigh, "I don't know if I'll ever see her again."

They finished up their practice session and headed back to the apartment. As Danny fixed himself some eggs on the Scary Stove, he ran over the beach conversation in his head.

His brothers were right. All the girls he'd dated last year were nice, nice, nice. The kind of girls you bring home to Mom with diamonds on their fingers. Nice was nice, he supposed.

Was it that simple? Was he attracted to Raven because she was "bad"? Because she had piercings and dyed hair and torn jeans? Or maybe because of the way she called him a "cool cat"?

Well . . . maybe it *was* that simple.

She seemed so *together*. Confident. Sexy. A girl with direction. All she had to do was point her skateboard and roll. So smooth.

Those eyes. That beautiful face. And yeah, that body. She wore that tight tank top real well.

But the eyes sealed it for him. Danny was drawn into them like a ship into a reef. Bottom line, he simply couldn't get Raven out of his head.

And the best part about that? He didn't want to.

*   *   *

37

Danny got off work close to eleven that night. It had been a long day, over ten hours schlepping heart attacks around the restaurant. He'd done better, however, in all areas. He messed up only one order and bagged nearly thirty bucks in tips. Plus he didn't get run over by oversized skate rats.

He walked down the boardwalk toward the apartment. It wasn't a bad walk. It would take him less than twenty minutes. After a day trapped in the Palace, the fresh air smelled positively wonderful.

The boards were growing deserted at this time of night. Danny could hear the surf pounding the shore, the breeze in his ears. Peaceful.

Then he heard something else. Behind him.

The clatter of small wheels on the boardwalk.

Skateboard wheels.

Before he could turn around, they were all around him. Screaming, laughing, slapping their boards against the planks beneath them. Danny recognized Doberman before the big guy slapped him playfully on the back.

"Hey, it's the punk-rock pretty boy!" he jeered. Doberman slowed down and turned a semicircle around Danny. "What, no ketchup tonight?"

Danny smirked coolly, but adrenaline pumped through his insides. Would Doberman be itching for another fight? And where was Raven? Danny looked around. He didn't see her. Just Doberman, Skunk, and the other two.

"So what's up, pretty boy?" Doberman asked sarcastically.

"Nothing," Danny replied. "You have another quiz for me?"

Doberman cackled, his shark-tooth earring dancing below his earlobe. "Not tonight, buddy. We have things to do. We're—"

"Very bored," came a familiar voice from behind them. Just then Raven skated between the pair, smoothly dragging her finger along Danny's jaw.

"C'mon, Raven." Doberman grunted. "We've got places to be." Doberman flashed his vampiric grin at Danny. "Later, pretty boy. Don't hurt yourself."

Doberman kicked away from him, his wheels rattling. The others followed him down the boardwalk, continuing their barking and catcalling over again. Danny sighed. Looked like they'd forgot about him. Which was just fine.

"Want some?"

Danny blinked. Raven was still there, slowly circling him on her board. She held out a half-gone lollipop, offering. And did she look fantastic. Her hair was pulled into spiky little pigtails, giving her a cool, girlish look. She wore the same torn jeans but with a tight, Lycra tie-dyed shirt that showed off her belly. A ring glinted in her navel.

"Hel-lo?" Raven called, waving the lollipop in front of Danny's face.

Danny blinked. "Sorry. It's been a long day. And night."

Be cool, he told himself. *Don't act like a dork. And don't sound nervous.*

Yeah, right.

"You work all day and all night?" she probed, returning the lollipop to her mouth. Her lips were bright red from it.

"Have to pay the rent," Danny said with a shrug.

She smiled, talking through the pop. "How did you know that song yesterday?"

Danny smiled back. Again he shrugged. "I don't know. I just did."

"You like punk music?" Raven gently pushed her board along as they walked. Danny noticed she was barefoot. Her toes were painted crimson. The soles of her feet were black with soot.

"I like every kind of music," Danny replied. "You name it, I probably have it."

"Calypso," Raven said immediately.

"Huh?"

"Calypso," she repeated, chuckling. "Harry Belafonte. It's a kind of music."

Danny laughed as well. "I guess I missed that kind."

Raven shook her head, tsking. "And you said you had it all."

Danny noticed Raven sizing him up. A wave of nervousness gripped him. He felt like a dork in his work clothes: black trousers and white button-down. He looked like, well, like an off-duty waiter. Raven didn't seem to care.

"I do . . . mostly," Danny replied, clearing his throat. *I sound like a moron!* "I listen to the Dustmites sometimes when I'm warming up for volleyball."

Raven's grin was incandescent. "Aha!" she said, holding up the lollipop as if to point to a lightbulb above her head. "I get it now. It's a bad-man, super-jock thing."

"I look like a jock to you?" Danny asked. He never thought of himself as a jock.

"Nope," Raven confirmed. "But guys who listen to punk music—or heavy metal, or grunge, or rap-metal; you name it—before they do something physical are usually trying to be meaner and more macho than they really are."

Danny chuckled. "I get it. I'm basically this clean-cut but wildly insecure jock wanna-be. Right?"

"You said it, not me," Raven replied. She offered the lollipop again. "Sure you don't want some? I'm gonna toss it."

Danny hesitated, and she met his eyes. Her gaze didn't waver. Which meant he couldn't let his waver either. A smirk slowly played across her face. "I don't have cooties."

Danny smiled and took the lollipop. He casually—extremely casually, he thought—put it in his mouth. It was warm and wet but tasted like a strawberry lollipop should taste. The stick just below the pop was frayed and wet. He swirled it around his mouth and pulled it out.

"Nope," he said. "No cooties."

Raven reached out and took the pop back. She returned it to her mouth. "So what's your name?" she asked.

"Danny," he replied, licking the strawberry from his lips. "Danny Ford. You're Raven, right?"

"No, just Raven," she said playfully.

Up ahead of them the sound of clattering wheels grew louder. Danny's heart sank. *Great,* he thought. *Here comes the Charm Squad again.*

Doberman, Skunk, and the other, unknown punks skated out of the dark. Doberman eyed Danny suspiciously, as if he was trespassing on private property.

"C'mon, Raven," Doberman ordered. "Let's jam. It's getting late."

"Past your bedtime?" Danny asked, hoping the comment didn't get him killed. But he wanted Doberman to know that he wasn't intimidated . . . even though he was.

"Watch it, pretty boy," Doberman said gravely. "You haven't earned the right to bust my chops." He nodded at Raven. "She's the only thing keeping you alive right now."

Danny looked at her. She didn't say a word.

What does that mean? he wondered.

"Leave the geek alone, Rave," Skunk said in disgust.

"Yeah, he's tired," Doberman added, looking Danny over from head to toe. "Like, *really* tired."

Danny rolled his eyes. "Yeah, I'm just a frat-boy-in-waiting."

"Gotta go, Danny," Raven said, stepping on her board and waving her little buh-bye wave.

Danny waved back. "Thanks for the lollipop."

"Anytime," Raven replied, but she was already turning away, pumping her bare foot against the boardwalk, picking up speed.

Soon the sound of clattering wheels faded away, and Danny was by himself. He let out a long sigh.

"Wow," he whispered, tasting sweet strawberry.

Four

T HE NEXT DAY Danny floated through work. Heart attacks and lipsticks flew to the tables almost on their own . . . which was bad since several of the orders went to tables they weren't supposed to.

Danny shook himself out of his stupor, apologized, set things right, then drifted back into his own little world. Luckily none of the customers turned out to be jerks. All they wanted was their food, not a fight.

Danny couldn't help it. He couldn't stop thinking about Raven.

This is amazing, he thought. *I've never felt like this about anyone before. Especially someone I don't really know.*

When he'd returned home last night, he slipped a Dustmites CD into the boom box just to see if he could read something into the music and learn more about Raven. But it was useless. The Dustmites were loud and illogical. A guy's band. They spoke of rebellion and anger and angst. That was the stuff that every punk rocker spoke of. There was nothing really unique that seemed to apply to Raven.

After a few songs, however, Johnny got so PO'd about the noise that he yanked the plug on the boom box.

Danny didn't care. He wasn't sure why he was so drawn to Raven. Well, duh, she was gorgeous. Of course. That helped. But there was something else. He couldn't put his finger on it. A connection between them somehow. She wasn't like other girls. But that went even beyond the color streaks in her hair. She wasn't even like other punks.

Doberman was your typical punk, Danny figured. He yelled, he screamed, he bullied. But there wasn't much more going on there.

Raven was playful. Or at least, she was playful last night. The lollipop thing was something Danny wouldn't soon forget.

So what was it? He'd had his crushes over the years, like any guy. And the girls he'd dated had something going. Enough that he found them both attractive and interesting. But none of them stuck.

What are you talking about, "stuck"? he berated himself. *You've crossed paths with this girl twice, both times by chance. You're not dating her, you don't know her last name, and you never will. So stop thinking about her like she's someone you've been with for three years!*

Danny knew better. This wasn't some random obsession. He didn't have them. Except for his music, he didn't obsess about anything. Now that Raven had come home to roost in his mind, he knew she wouldn't be leaving anytime soon. He was all too aware of what she gave him: direction. He knew which way to go. He knew what he wanted. No wandering. No waffling. Raven was a magnetic north as true as anything he'd ever felt. And it felt good.

He had to talk to her again. But how? Even if he could find her, what was he going to do—take her to a movie? *Lame*. Plus her friends didn't exactly make her accessible. They thought Danny was a total preppy geek fool frat boy. Or something like that.

So how did he make this happen?

Maybe I'm not supposed to, he thought dejectedly as he picked up two more plates full of food. *Maybe I should just forget about Raven and stick to the nice, bland girls I'm used to.*

He served the food to table four. He reversed the plates between the two customers—a guy and girl about his age—but at least all the right food made it to the right table.

Danny looked at the girl he'd just served. She was cute. Brown eyes, blond ponytail, smooth tan legs, a hot pink beach pullover. That was the kind of girl he was used to. And the guy with her? Not that far from himself. Clean-cut. Calm. Courteous. The guy didn't flinch when Danny mixed up their food.

What's wrong with a girl like that? he asked himself. Nothing. She was cute. And probably a lot of fun.

There were hundreds of girls just like her, sunning themselves on the beach. Riding the merry-go-round on the pier. Strolling up and down the boardwalk. All he had to do was walk up and say, "Hi!"

But Danny didn't want to. He'd taken out girls like that his whole dating career (if you could call what he had a career). It was time to follow his heart.

He wanted to be with Raven.

Somehow. Someway.

He would make it happen.

Danny got off work close to ten-thirty. After three days he was starting to get into the routine. And he was getting better at the waiter stuff. Jabba didn't say a word to him all day, which he took to be a good sign.

Now it was time to go home. He wanted to watch the last few innings of the Dodgers game, then sleep.

But when he stepped out onto the boardwalk, he saw her immediately.

Raven.

She leaned against the railing on the far side. She had laid her skateboard on the railing, chassis up. She idly spun the wheels, as if waiting for something. Or someone.

Me? Danny wondered . . . but didn't dare hope.

She smiled when she spotted him, offering one of her playful little waves.

Now's your chance, he told himself. *Get moving. Talk to her. You may never see her again.* He paused. *But above all, be cool, dude.*

Danny smiled back and crossed the boardwalk. Raven looked as hot as ever. Her hair hung down straight tonight, the pink streaks fading into the light brown like disappearing ink.

It was really her. No Doberman, no Skunk, no skate rats hovering. Just her.

"Hi," Danny said casually, trying not to seem too happy or too blasé.

"What's up, Danny," she replied, spinning a skateboard wheel. "Fancy meeting you here."

"I'm always here," he said, nodding at the Jabba's Palace sign. "There's no escaping Jabba."

"I know—his burgers are killer."

"Literally," Danny muttered. Was he trying too hard? He couldn't stop staring at her eyes.

"Can you get me a discount sometime?"

"Anytime," he promised. "Three percent."

"Three percent?" Raven rolled her eyes. "What's the point?"

Danny shrugged. "Jabba doesn't like to give up the pennies. I get free fries and Fizz, but everything else is cash-and-carry. But if you ever come in, I can get you a good table. And guarantee good service."

Raven smiled and nodded. "Yeah, it's good to

know people on the inside. Maybe I'll stop in. But Doberman and Skunk will have to wait outside. They got booted from that place last week. They're banned for the summer."

Good, Danny thought. "What did they do?"

"Nothing," Raven replied, her voice growing angry. "They were just themselves. Jabba kicked them out because of the way they dressed. How they looked. That jerk should talk."

"Yeah, Jabba's lots of laughs," Danny said.

Raven looked him over. "You on your way home?"

Danny nodded. "I was."

Raven paused, then asked, "You want company?"

Danny blinked. His stomach flip-flopped. *Are you kidding? Are you nuts? Are you serious?*

"Sure," he said, trying to sound calm.

"Cool." Raven dropped her board and slowly pushed it along as Danny walked.

Danny eyed her. "No parties tonight?"

Raven shrugged. "I dunno. Why do you ask?"

"Where's the rest of the pack? Doberman get his shots today or something?"

Raven snickered. "Very funny. No, they're off doing some macho thing somewhere. I don't really know. Actually, they're the reason I wanted to see you tonight."

"Really?"

"I wanted to apologize for them," she continued. "Especially Doberman. They can be real jerks."

"No problem," Danny replied, shrugging. "I've seen worse." But Danny actually felt like saying, *I'd use a word so much nastier than* jerks *that I'd have to be bleeped.*

"They can *be* worse," Raven countered. "The song thing really threw Doberman. Not many people stand up to His Alpha Maleness, but you did."

Danny met her gaze. "Is that why you talk to me?"

Raven smiled. "Don't you want to talk to me?"

"It's about the only thing I want to do these days," he replied, instantly regretting his honesty. *Idiot, moron, dweeb!*

Raven only laughed, pushing her board along with her bare feet. "I don't know why I talk to you. I mean, we're both thinking the same thing: totally different people, totally nothing in common, totally useless."

"I guess," Danny answered. "Or not."

"I'll take not," Raven replied. "I don't know. Maybe it's because you stood up to Doberman. Maybe I think you're brave. Or reckless. Maybe I like your taste in music. Or . . . maybe I just think you're cute."

Danny's heart skipped a beat. She actually thought he was cute? Unbe-freakin'-lievable. He struggled to keep his voice from cracking. "I'm cute?"

"For a frat-boy-in-waiting," Raven replied, smiling.

"I'm kind of shocked," Danny said cautiously. "I

mean, I never would have guessed. I mean, I hoped. I mean, I never figured a girl like you would ever like a guy like me."

Raven chuckled. "That's three I-means. I think I see what you mean."

"You do?"

"Well . . ." Raven stroked her chin. "What exactly is a girl like me?"

Watch yourself, dude, he thought. Just be cool. Speak the truth. How bad could it be? "You seem like you have it together. Like you know exactly what you like. I'm like a thousand other guys here for the summer. I figured you'd like a guy who's different." *Say it,* he told himself. *Say what you're really thinking.* "I figured you'd like a guy like Doberman. I figured you were with him."

Her expression darkened. "That was seven 'likes.' And no," she added curtly. "But I guess what you see is what you get."

Uh-oh. Was she mad? Had he said something wrong? "What do you mean by that?"

"You see my hair, my earrings, my tattoo, and you automatically think I must be with Doberman."

Danny nodded. "He sure acted like you were together."

"Looks can be deceiving, Danny," she replied, staring him down.

"You have a tattoo?" Danny asked.

Raven nodded.

"Where? Or aren't I allowed to ask?"

She looked at him slyly. "You can ask. Who

knows if I'll tell? I wouldn't want you to get the wrong idea about me."

"What idea is that?" Danny asked, kicking a crumpled paper cup and trying to appear nonchalant. He didn't know what to do with himself. *Just walk, dude.*

"You're obviously looking at me and assuming I am how I look." She popped a wheelie with her board and slammed the front end down with a loud *whap*. "I must be a drug-doing, class-cutting, draft-dodging, mosh-pitting sleaze who likes to hang out in the backs of vans at Nine Inch Nails concerts."

"You mean you aren't?" Danny chuckled. "Darn."

Raven tried to keep a straight face, but a smirk crept through.

"What are you, then?" Danny probed. "And I'm not asking to patronize you. I'm asking because I really want to know. I'm actually relieved that you aren't a draft-dodging whatever. I'm not interested in that girl."

Raven shrugged. "My guess is I'm just like you. I hate school, but I get straight As. I hate the idea of college, but I want to go. And I consider myself to be the most stable person in my family even though I'm the only one with multiple body piercings and a tattoo."

"And dyed hair," Danny added.

Raven shook her head. "Nope. Both my mom and my older sister dye their hair. I'm just the one who chose streaks of dark pink."

"If you're so normal, why do you dress the way you do?" Danny asked.

53

"Because I like it," she said, as if it was the most logical thing in the world. "I like my friends. I like messing with people's heads. But only the people who think they're better than me because of the way I dress. I mean, I get looks of contempt from all the bottle bikini blondes my age because their boyfriends are checking me out. But because I ride a board and wear tight tops, I must be a slut. Meanwhile they aren't within a hundred slots of my class rank."

Danny nodded. "I get it. But you're wrong too. You assume by the way I look—"

"Neo—frat boy?" she interjected.

"Exactly," Danny continued. "You assume that since I have this look, I must be a college-bound-and-gagged brownnoser from the right side of the tracks."

"You're not?" Raven asked, eyeing him suspiciously.

"I could go to college," Danny said, shrugging. "But I don't know if it's in the cards. My grades are so-so. I have absolutely no interest in anything whatsoever except listening to music. I can't play an instrument. I can't do calculus. I can't write a coherent sentence. My dad's blue-collar, so I don't have any guarantees to fall back on. No family business to inherit. Basically I'm taking things one day at a time, hoping to be inspired by something. Anything." Danny sighed. "I guess the bottom line is that we're not the people we think we are."

"Looks can be deceiving," Raven echoed.

"Exactly," he replied flatly.

Neither of them spoke for a moment. They soaked up the finality of what they'd just said. Finally Raven turned to Danny. Her smirk had returned. "Even long, lingering looks?"

"What do you—," Danny began, but he stopped when he saw her. Really saw her.

Raven stared at him. Openly. Blatantly. Her eyes opened up and took him in, offering him a glimpse at the real person underneath all the hardware and color. She was like him, tender and vulnerable and fragile and, bottom line, just looking for the right person to open up to.

Danny couldn't speak. He didn't know how. After all, how did you respond when you got something you really wanted? When something turned out exactly the way you wanted it? Words could wreck the moment.

"You want a ride home?" Raven asked finally.

Danny blinked himself out of his trance. "What do you mean?"

Raven gestured at her skateboard.

"On that?" he asked, skeptical.

Raven slid her bare feet forward, offering Danny half of the board. "Hop on," she said. "But you have to get close."

Danny smiled. "I dunno. . . ."

Raven held up her hands. "Hey, if you want to walk, that's cool. I'm just trying to be nice."

"Okay, okay," Danny replied quickly. "I'm not one to turn down charity."

He awkwardly stepped up onto the board, first

one foot, then adjusting for the other foot when he realized just how close he would have to get to her.

"Closer," she urged.

Danny slipped in behind her, balancing precariously on the narrow skateboard. It was so awkward, but so nice. And so close.

"You have to put your arms around me, Danny," she said, her voice suddenly soft. "Otherwise you'll fall off. I promise I won't take it personally."

Danny did as he was told. He could smell the sweet shampoo in her hair. The faint scent of perfume on her neck, brand unknown. It was maddening. He tentatively slipped his hands around her waist. She grabbed them and pulled him closer, planting his palms flat on her belly.

Danny's heart pounded. His ears felt red-hot. Her body was so soft, the fabric of her top so smooth and warm.

"So, uh . . . how does this work?" he asked lamely.

"Just give us a push," Raven whispered, looking over her shoulder at him.

That move brought their lips within inches of each other. All Danny had to do was bend forward the slightest bit, and he would be kissing her. Her lips were moist, her smirk obvious. It was as if she was waiting for him to do it.

He couldn't.

Not yet, he thought numbly. *I'll blow it. I'll do or say something stupid, and she'll totally lose interest in me. She'll see what a dork I really am.*

Then another voice piped up in his head.

Dude, be cool. You're standing on a skateboard with a beautiful girl. She's giving you the go-ahead to plant a sweet one on her. But you shouldn't. Take your time. Don't let her make the play. Just be yourself, and she'll be back.

Who was *that?* Danny wondered. Obviously he knew it was himself, but it was a side of himself he'd never heard before. A side that was mostly instinct. And totally calm under fire. He was glad to hear it.

"You have to make the first move, Danny," Raven prodded. "Or we'll be here all night."

Danny slowly nodded. He dipped one foot off the board and pushed. They started moving down the sidewalk. It was a slow ride, but one of the most intense thrills Danny had ever experienced.

Maybe this is the kind of social stupidity that has been holding me back for so long, he thought. *Letting appearances dictate my actions.* If so, this was a good start, he figured. Why? Because riding that skateboard down the boardwalk felt so right.

It wasn't long before Danny's apartment building came into view. Not nearly long enough, if you asked him.

He spotted two feet sticking over the railing of their balcony, three floors above the boardwalk. Johnny.

Ignore him, Danny told himself.

"This is me," he said into Raven's ear.

They came to a halt. Danny reluctantly stepped

off the skateboard. "Thanks for the ride, Raven."

"Anytime." She smiled playfully.

They were silent for a moment, fidgeting. Should he do something more? Danny wondered. Kiss her good night? Shake her hand?

"Well . . . good night," he finally said.

"Later," she replied. Then quickly added, "Say . . ."

"Yeah?"

Her tone was back to all business. "There's a bonfire party on the beach this Saturday night, off Wayfarer Avenue. Starts around nine. The whole world will be there. Wanna come?"

Danny smiled—then paused. His two friends from home, Scott Walsh and Charlie McCay, were coming to hang for the weekend. Crashing on the floor. Sleeping on the beach. Napping in the late afternoon. Guy stuff. "I have friends visiting this weekend. They're coming Saturday afternoon."

"Bring them," Raven said simply.

Danny smiled. "I'll try."

"Try harder." Raven smacked him on the rear end, giggled, and skated off into the darkness.

Wow, he thought. Nice. In all, Danny couldn't have imagined a finer ending to a better night. Until . . .

From above him on the balcony came the humiliating echo of Johnny's and Kevin's hootchy-kootchy kissing sounds.

What I Found in a Guy!
by Raven

1. Beneath the guise of a preppy lurks . . . a rebel! Danny's a little square around the edges, but he's totally cool.

2. Hair that looks good without gel, mousse, and/or gelatin.

3. Someone who I can really talk to.

4. A great listener.

5. An even better kisser (I can tell).

6. Beautiful deep green eyes that turn me to mush.

Five

"GEE, SHE LOOKS like a very nice girl, Dan-o," Johnny commented as Danny shut the apartment door. The odor of stale garlic hit his nose. An open pizza box sat on the kitchen table, surrounded by empty Fizz bottles.

"You always spy on people, Johnny?" Danny replied angrily. He tossed his wallet and keys on the table. Wasn't it enough that he had to smell grease all day at work?

"Not spying, dude," Johnny countered from the ratty couch. He and Kevin were munching pizza while watching the Dodgers game on TV. "I was taking in the night surf on the balcony, and you just happened to cross my path."

Danny nodded. "You must have gotten a real good look at Raven from three stories up in the dark."

Johnny and Kevin glanced at each other. *"Raven?"* they blurted out simultaneously.

A wave of rage coursed through Danny. "Yeah. That's her name. Do you have a problem with it?"

"Oooh, do I have a problem with it?" Johnny repeated in a mock-afraid voice. "What is this, dialogue by De Niro?"

"You talkin' to me?" Kevin asked, snickering. He tore off a piece of pizza and tossed the crust across the room at the open box. It ricocheted off the kitchen table and landed in the far corner. Kevin made no effort to retrieve it.

"At least her name has style," Danny muttered, slumping into a kitchen chair. The ancient metal frame of the seat groaned with the effort. "Unlike, say, Danny or Kevin or John . . . or *Jane*."

"So what's your point?" Kevin asked, returning his gaze to the TV.

"The point is, I like this girl," Danny said. "Hopefully I'll be seeing a lot more of her. I don't need to hear hootchy-kootchy noises every time I say good night to her."

"So sensitive," Johnny teased. "You won't have any time to see her anyway. Aren't Tweedledee and Tweedledum coming up this weekend?"

"Yeah, *Scott* and *Charlie* are coming. I'm gonna take them to a bonfire party Saturday night. I'll see Raven there too. What's the big deal?"

"Bonfire?" Kevin asked, sitting up. "What bonfire?"

"On the beach, down by Wayfarer Avenue," Danny replied smugly. "What? Weren't you studs invited? The nerve!"

"Oh, man," Johnny said, his voice tight. "We

have to listen to this attitude all summer? No way. No way, man."

"I'm just giving what I'm getting, John Boy," Danny said. "You want to bust my chops about Raven and my friends, fine. But I'm not gonna just sit and take it."

"Can anyone go to this bonfire?" Kevin asked, ignoring his brothers' conversation. "It sounds cool."

"You can both go if you want," Danny said with a shrug. "You've been doing the monk thing so far. You won't meet anyone that way."

Johnny laughed in that annoying, older-brother way. "You meet one skate rat named after a demon bird with earrings all over her face, and suddenly you're Social Sally?"

Rage boiled in Danny once again. "She doesn't have any face piercings, Johnny. She's just as normal as you or me."

Johnny laughed again. "Yeah, I bet. Just wait until Scott and Charlie meet her. That'll be real cool. Their laces are so straight, their mothers probably iron them. They'll really like your new rebel friend."

Danny couldn't take it anymore. He stood up and savagely pointed a finger at his older brother. "That's just like you. Make a stupid remark like that when you haven't even met the girl. Scott and Charlie will be fine with her. You know why? Because Raven isn't like you. She'll talk to anyone, regardless of how they dress."

Johnny eyed Danny's grease-stained work clothes. "Obviously."

Danny left his brothers to their baseball game—a game he would've liked to watch. But he couldn't stand being around Johnny anymore. Sure, brothers fought, he reasoned, but Johnny had crossed the line.

No one ever busts his chops about Jane, Danny thought. *She and Johnny have been together for years. And she's as cold as ice to everyone but him. I don't know how he puts up with her.*

He wondered if that was why Johnny was acting the way he was. Maybe Johnny realized it was his turn to bust on the girlfriend for once.

Danny exited the apartment building and crossed the boardwalk to the beach entrance ramp. He kicked off his shoes and carried them. The sand felt cool and soft against his skin. His feet ached from the day's work. Danny curled his toes and flexed them in the sand, letting the stress flow out of them.

Stress, Danny thought glumly. *I'm at the hottest beach on the West Coast. I just met an even hotter girl who seems to like me. And I have stress. Ha. Some vacation.*

Remember the volleyball tournament, he told himself. That's why he was here. Things like his job, the beach, and Raven had to be secondary to the tournament.

Yeah, right.

Raven was a part of every thought.

The surf pounded the sand in reply. A cool Pacific breeze fluttered through his hair. The stars were bright in the sky. The beach was quiet. Peaceful. He wished Raven was with him.

Enjoy it now, he thought. *Once the weekend rolls around, it's all over.*

Danny had lied to Johnny. He truly wasn't sure how Scott and Charlie would react to Raven. Johnny was right about one thing: His friends were straitlaced tighter than an old lady's girdle.

What if they acted like Johnny? What if they wouldn't accept Raven?

Then, Danny thought grimly, *this bonfire party could get very, very ugly. . . .*

Six

T HE BONFIRE RAGED eight feet into the night
air. The coals at the base of the fire crackled
with waves of yellow-red heat. Embers and smoke
floated into the star-filled sky. No one could get
within five feet because it was so hot. And there
was no sign of the fire dying since a huge stack of
firewood (and some old wooden deck furniture)
was stacked nearby. It was a disco inferno if there
ever was one.

Danny would've been shocked to hear any disco
music, however. A roofless Land Rover was parked
several yards away on the sand. Its muscular stereo
blasted what Danny recognized immediately as the
Farm Animals' rap-metal version of Led Zeppelin's
"Ramble On." All bass, no prisoners.

A hundred kids of various ages, sizes, and appearance jostled back and forth around the fire,
from skate rats to trust-fund brats. Danny, his

brothers, and Scott and Charlie had arrived just after nine o'clock. The scene was red-hot in all ways.

"Nice," Kevin commented, surveying the party carnage. "This is my kind of beach."

Just then a long-haired, gray-bearded guy in a tie-dyed T-shirt and brown shorts shuffled up to them. "Dudes . . . free Fizz over in those coolers." He giggled, showing crooked teeth. "If you're into that sort of thing."

He tee-hee-heed away.

"That guy had to be in his sixties," Johnny said, staring after him.

"I think there's a lot about that guy that screams sixties," Kevin replied, laughing. He took a few steps in the direction of the coolers, then turned. "I'm going. Who needs one?"

"I'll go with you," Johnny replied, shrugging. "Better than standing here like a wallflower."

The two Ford brothers crossed the sand, entered the crowd, and disappeared.

"This is pretty cool," Scott Walsh observed. His curly brown hair was cut close to his scalp. His blue eyes glistened in the firelight. Danny thought his Polo shirt and Abercrombie & Fitch shorts seemed more suited to a tennis club than a beach party. "Not a bad way to spend the summer, Dan."

"No kidding," Charlie McKay added. His tousled blond hair and blue eyes were very California-beachy-keen casual, but his shorts were pressed, and his Teva sandals were brand-new.

68

His friends had arrived on schedule that evening. Danny was glad to see them, though they had only a couple of hours to catch up before it was time to go to the bonfire. Danny was able to scam a couple of free hours from Jabba's. It was Saturday night, after all, and his friends were in town. His overdressed, underrelaxed friends. But hey, nobody was perfect.

Danny slipped a casual hand in his own beat-up cargo shorts. He couldn't imagine dressing up for a beach party. Thus his Dustmites concert shirt and bare feet. It was the beach, not the club.

Which has nothing to do with trying to impress/charm/dazzle Raven, he told himself. *Absolutely not. No way. I'm not one to judge a person by their appearance. You own a few Polo shirts yourself, buddy boy,* he reminded himself.

Danny quickly forgot his hypocrisy before it could put a serious crimp in his party-go-nuts attitude. He was there to have a good time, after all. And see Raven.

And that's just what he was doing at that moment.

She was on the other side of the bonfire, near the Land Rover. A dozen skate rats surrounded her. Doberman, Skunk, and the others he'd run into were there, plus a platoon of others that he'd never seen before.

Raven spotted him. Smiled. Waved him over. She swayed with the music and continued her conversation with another girl.

Uh-oh.

She wanted him to come over. Her friends, Doberman in particular, wouldn't like that.

Dude, the girl you're totally hot for just invited you over, a voice in his head piped up. *Don't be a dweeb. Go!*

"I have to go check on something, guys," Danny said to Scott and Charlie, his gaze never leaving Raven. "I'll be right back."

"Is that her?" Scott asked, squinting through the fire's glare.

"Which one?" piped Charlie. "They all look the same."

Danny sighed. Oh, well. Of course they would want to meet Raven. Johnny and Kevin had made sure earlier that his friends knew all about Danny's new main squeeze-to-be. Anything to make his life difficult.

"That's her on the right," Danny relented, pointing her out. "The one with the tank top and torn jeans."

"And the belly-button ring," Scott added, his smirk growing by the second. "Verrrry nice."

Danny spun on his friend. "So she has a navel piercing. So what? You have Yoda boxer shorts."

Charlie cackled. "Yeah, but Scott doesn't hang them from his belly button."

"So that's it," Danny muttered, shaking his head in frustration. "You guys are going to be just like Johnny. I really like this girl. Can't you just be cool for ten minutes?"

Scott and Charlie shared a look. Then Charlie glanced at his watch. "Gee, Danny, I don't know. That's a tall order."

"You can do better than her," Scott said, glancing at Raven. "Why go for the most radical girl on the beach?"

Charlie laughed. "She looks kind of scary, dude."

"That's it," Danny snapped. "I'm going over to see her. You want to come, come. I'll introduce you. If not, I'm sure Johnny'll be back in a few minutes with more funny things to say about me. What's it going to be?"

Charlie sighed and crossed his arms. "Whatever."

Scott shrugged. "Go, then."

Danny turned away from his friends. He imagined their stares burning into his back as he crossed the sand to Raven, but that was just the heat from the bonfire.

They think I'm ditching them, Danny thought glumly. *Fine. Let them think that. I'm just going to say hello to Raven. Five minutes. Then I'll go back to them.*

Danny even believed it.

"Hey," she said.

"Hey, back," he said.

Raven looked amazing in the fire's glow. Her features were cast in flickering shadows. Her hair hung straight along her cheeks. Her eyes seemed to dance as she sized him up. Through it all she never stopped her rhythmic swaying to the music.

Danny gulped. *Be cool,* the voice told him. *You're just a regular guy, and she's your garden-variety gorgeous amazing wonderful unattainable girl. And she wants to talk to you.*

71

No sweat.

"Cool party," he said calmly, offering a slight smile.

"Not really," she replied, shrugging. "Want to go for a walk?"

Danny blinked. "Um . . . sure."

"Come on," she muttered, grabbing his hand and pulling him toward the dark surf.

"Yo, Raven!" came a familiar bellow.

Uh-oh. Danny closed his eyes and whispered a curse. *Here we go again.*

Raven turned impatiently at the voice. *"What?"*

It was indeed Doberman. He held a bottle of something in his hand. Danny couldn't tell what from the angle. He and his spiked hair, shark-tooth earring, and ripped clothes were silhouetted in the firelight. Danny could also see the muscles and veins flexing in Doberman's arms. He didn't have to see his face to know the big guy's vampiric teeth were flashing too.

"What's with punk-rock boy?" Doberman asked indignantly. "Suddenly we're all second-class citizens?"

Raven sighed wearily and shook her head. "Nothing so melodramatic, Dobie. Just plain old boring."

Doberman's head tilted as if he hadn't heard her right. *"Boring?* Raven, you're holding hands with *boring.* That guy represents everything stompable in this whole world. You hate guys like him for breakfast."

Adrenaline rose in Danny. He felt Raven's hand tighten around his own.

"Times change, Dobie," she replied haughtily. "And looks can be deceiving."

Doberman chuckled bitterly. "You're right, Rave. A Dustmites T-shirt doesn't make him worth even one of your glances."

Raven laughed. "Keep it up, Doberman. You'll be a poet yet." She tugged on Danny's arm. "Come on, let's go."

"Where are we going?" Danny asked lamely, trotting to keep up as she headed down the beach.

Raven led him along the fringe of the surf line, the sand growing wet and cold under Danny's feet. "Destination unknown, Danny. Let's make it up as we go, okay?"

Danny smiled. "I've been doing that my whole life."

The bonfire quickly became a faint glow. The sound of the heavy bass was replaced by the pounding surf. Raven never let go of his hand, and Danny had no plans to argue.

Soon they came to a jetty—an outcropping of rocks and massive concrete pilings that ran so far out into the ocean, it was swallowed up. The waves slammed against the man-made barrier, sending up dramatic sprays of foam.

Finally Raven let go of his hand and scrambled to the top of one of the concrete pilings, perching there like a gargoyle. Danny followed suit on one of the rocks, careful not to cut his bare feet on the rough, slick surface.

"Why did you leave your friends?" he asked. He could see her profile against the starlit sky, a perfect black outline of beauty. *We're all the same in the dark,* he thought happily.

"I'm with them all the time," Raven said. "They're my friends, but they all talk about the same things day after day. Skateboarding, partying, making out, whatever. My girlfriends are even worse. Sometimes I just have to get away."

"Am I different enough for you?" Danny asked carefully.

Raven chuckled. "You're not all that different, Danny. Just a change of speed."

Danny felt a wave of warmth flow through him, and he wished Raven wasn't so far away on her concrete piling. "Speed has never been my problem," he said softly. "It's direction that I have trouble with."

"Me too," Raven replied, nodding. "Sometimes I feel like I'm floating out there on the ocean. My friends spin around me at a hundred miles an hour. But it's all random. There's no land to shoot for."

Danny couldn't help smiling. She'd nailed it right on the head. That was his life to a T. "Seems like everyone I know is shooting by, but they all have places to go. My brother Kevin has art. Johnny has college. What do I have?"

"Freedom," Raven said firmly.

"I don't know about that," Danny replied with a

sigh. "I don't feel very free slinging burgers at Jabba's. I don't feel free when my parents and relatives ask me what I want to do with my life. An answer like 'be free' doesn't cut it with them."

"People can't tell you how to live," Raven said, her voice gaining a momentary edge. "It's hard enough just being yourself. You think my family likes the torn jeans and hot tops I wear? The earrings? But there comes a point where you have to say, 'I don't care what you think. This is me.' "

"Even if you don't know who you are?" Danny replied.

"You can't force direction, Danny," Raven countered, slipping off the piling and silently hitting the sand. She took a step toward him, and her voice grew tender. "It's a little bit like falling for someone. It just comes out of nowhere, and all you can do is go with it."

Danny's stomach fluttered. Maybe it was Raven's tone. Maybe it was the beautiful shape of her silhouette. Maybe it was her words. But Danny had never felt so right with anyone. She knew what was burrowing inside him, eating away. She knew how to feed it. Suddenly Danny didn't feel so alone about the future because out here, among the random waves of the ocean, the future didn't matter. He wasn't the only one floating through life's gray areas. The irony of it all was that this beautiful randomness, this great discovery, now gave him a sense of direction. And everything pointed to Raven.

Without thinking, Danny stood from his rock, stepped forward, and kissed her.

He expected her to pull away. Smack him. Bite his lip and tell him to get lost.

But she didn't.

She grabbed handfuls of his T-shirt and pulled him closer. He wrapped his arms around her, feeling the warmth of her skin through tight fabric. Her lips were firm and alive against his own, and Danny realized that Raven was not only letting him kiss her, but she was kissing him back.

He never dreamed she would.

It was a long shot.

But she was.

And the whole world fell away until it was just him and her . . . and an amazing moment that he never wanted to end.

They didn't talk on their way back to the party. Their kiss simply broke, mutually, and they took each other's hand once again and walked.

It made sense. No one had to say anything.

Danny's head was swimming, pounding along like the endless surf. What did this mean? Were they a couple now? Danny hated words like that, the window dressing of relationships: couples, dating, communicating, all that.

Don't make a big deal of it, the inner voice told him. *You guys kissed, that's all. You connected.* People did it on first dates all the time. He watched TV. People did it in fifteen-second commercials. *We're a kissing society, and one kiss does not a destiny make.*

Danny knew he was downplaying it. He had to, for his own sanity. If he acknowledged his true feelings, he'd be hanging out in the wind. The sun had a funny way of rising and making people suddenly feel strange about what they did the night before. Who knew how Raven would treat him later? Was the kiss as amazing for her as it was for him?

Could she possibly feel as good as I do right now? he wondered.

No way. No chance. Impossible.

So Danny took it one step at a time. And buried all of his feelings under a bed of cool denial thick enough to sleep on.

Soon the bonfire came into view. The heavy bass thumped into his chest. The party was still rocking well. Danny spotted his brothers and friends talking to a group of girls near the Fizz coolers. Out of the corner of his eye he caught Raven staring at them.

"You want to meet them?" he asked.

Raven shrugged. "Okay. If you want to introduce me, that is . . ."

Careful, he warned himself. *That sounds like a verbal trap if I ever heard one.* "Sure. Come on."

They walked over to the group. Kevin caught Danny's eye and grinned. He then nudged Johnny and pointed at them. Johnny wore a bemused smile.

Just before they reached the group, Raven let go of Danny's hand. His palm felt cold without hers.

77

"Hey, everyone," Danny announced. "This is Raven."

"Hey," everyone replied.

Danny ran down the names for her, Johnny, Kevin, Scott, Charlie. The three girls they were talking to were Angie, Katherine, and Jean Marie. They all wore designer summer wear, makeup, and perfume. And they looked at Raven like she might pull a knife on them at any time.

After the intros there was an uncomfortable moment of silence.

Finally Kevin stepped forward and smiled. "So, Raven, why are you hanging out with my loser brother?"

"I dig charity cases," Raven replied, smiling herself.

"Hey—," Danny protested, but Raven nudged him.

The others turned back to their conversations, but Danny noticed a distinct air of resentment coming from his friends. Scott and Charlie made no effort to speak to Raven, even though the girls they were with were less than scintillating conversationalists.

Is it about how Raven looks? Danny wondered. *Or is it about the fact that I'd rather spend time with her than with them?*

A little of both, he figured.

It didn't matter. All Danny had to do was look at Raven and think about their kiss. When he did that, nothing else mattered.

"I hear you're an artist," Raven commented to Kevin. "What do you draw?"

Kevin spread his arms wide, grinning. "Everything. The world is my oyster, and I'm the grain of sand that becomes the pearl."

Raven giggled. Danny rolled his eyes. "I forgot to warn you about Kevin's uncanny ability to lay it on thick."

"With a shovel," Kevin added, nodding. He gestured at Raven's legs. "Those jeans are perfect. How long did it take you to get them to look like that?"

Raven glanced at the shreds of denim and shrugged. "Forever, I guess. I didn't tear any of those holes. They grew naturally and decayed rapidly. All I had to do was wear them a lot. And fall off my skateboard a lot."

"Cool," Kevin replied. "Air-conditioned, even."

Raven smiled. "Saves money on the designer labels."

Danny felt relief that Kevin seemed to be warming toward Raven. At least one of his brothers would give her the time of day. That it was Kevin didn't surprise him, though. His younger brother ran a little on the ragged edge himself, or at least he liked to think he did. The artist in him kept his mind open. And his wit sharp. It was a combination that Raven no doubt found easy to relate to.

Just as Danny started to relax, a racket erupted from the other side of the bonfire.

Loud voices. Laughter. Cursing. A new group of people had arrived at the party, coming up the beach from the pier. Danny didn't get a good look at them until they neared the fire, but he caught the expression on Doberman's face over by the Land Rover: disgust.

I guess I'm not the only one who makes Dobie sick, Danny thought.

There were thirteen of them, all of them obviously older, all of them obviously drunk. By their clothes and general attitude Danny could tell they were rich. But it was the leader of the pack who drew Danny's eye. He had to be about six-four in bare feet. His T-shirt and shorts hung easy on his massive, muscular frame, adding to his entire air of confidence. His shaggy, styled blond hair fell to his shoulders, and his perfect grin never wavered, staying bright and magnetic even as he insulted the lameness of the party. And he looked very familiar . . .

"Danger, everyone," the guy announced to his friends as he surveyed the crowd. "Looks like we've gone back in time to the tenth grade."

His friends laughed.

"How witty," Raven muttered. "Let's tap another keg."

Danny suddenly noticed Johnny at his side. His older brother glared at the pack leader, almost willing the guy to look at him.

"You recognize him?" Johnny whispered.

"He does look familiar," Danny replied, confirming his suspicions. "Who is he?"

"Tanner St. John," Kevin replied, giving the name all the reverence of a cockroach.

Recognition flooded Danny. Of course. Tanner

St. John, all-American and captain of the national-champion California University men's volleyball team. Six-four, two-ten, known for his three-foot vertical leap, a spike that could crack your skull, and an ego the size of southern California.

Johnny pointed out two other guys in Tanner's group. Arliss Neeson, a dark-haired, lantern-jawed guy who stared nails through you from under his thick black eyebrows. He was second-team all-American and once put an opposing player in the hospital for coming too far over the volleyball net. When the guy went up near the net, Arliss swept the guy's feet. He came down on his head.

The other was Shooter Ridge. He wore a ribbed tank top to show off the definition of his arms and chest. His jet black hair was parted at the side and molded into place by lots of hair spray. Every few minutes he absently ran a hand along each arm, as if to make sure the muscles there hadn't deteriorated.

"The team to beat in this summer's tournament," Kevin said grimly.

Danny took a deep breath. All of them were over six feet tall. All of them were lean and muscular, the classic volleyball build. And all of them played on a national-champion team.

"It's a cakewalk," Johnny scoffed, watching every move Tanner St. John made.

Sure, it is, Danny thought. *My brother, the optimist.*

Then Tanner St. John looked right at Johnny. Danny saw a flicker of recognition in the rowdy guy's eyes. Tanner nudged his teammates and gestured at Johnny. Then they marched toward the Fords. Danny stuck out his chest. He didn't have a real idea of the opposing players' size until they stopped a few feet in front of him. Johnny was the closest, at six-one. But Danny and Kevin hadn't topped out at six feet yet.

"I know you," Tanner said, his eyes smoldering. He brushed his long hair out of his face and smirked.

"Yeah," Johnny said, his voice even and confident. He glared right back.

Tanner stroked his chin, thinking. "Your name's Chevy, or Pontiac, or something."

"Ford." Johnny took a deep, agitated breath.

Tanner smiled and snapped his fingers. "Ford. That's the one. Yeah, CU tried to recruit you last spring. You choked at the tryout."

Danny saw the blood rise in his brother's face. Johnny bristled but kept his cool. "Funny. That's not how I remember it."

"It's a shame that you're in such denial," Tanner said, to the tittering delight of his friends. "I mean, it's never you, right? Let me guess. The balls were half flat, and the net was six inches higher than normal. Does that explain your pathetic excuse for a spike?"

"Nothing wrong with my spike, pal," Johnny replied. The muscles in his jaw flexed.

Tanner shrugged, as if to grant Johnny his opinion. "Sure. Not if you're going to play for East Podunk University. But the program at CU is a little more demanding." Tanner held his hand a few inches over Johnny's head, as if measuring. "You don't quite make the grade."

Johnny batted Tanner's hand away. A ripple of excitement went through the crowd.

Tanner's eyes went wide. He held up his struck hand as if it were a prize. His perfect teeth shone dully in the firelight. "He touched me. Did you see that? Did you see this guy touch me?"

"He definitely touched you," Arliss Neeson agreed, smiling savagely. He crossed his massive arms over his chest.

"You gonna stand for that, Tanner?" Shooter Ridge demanded, taking up station at Tanner's left shoulder. He looked like he wanted to drool.

"Do you know what happened to the last guy to touch me?" Tanner asked, his voice out of a bad Western.

"He got your phone number?" Kevin blurted out. He'd snuck in next to Johnny, which was easy since he only came up to his brother's shoulder.

The crowd burst out laughing, which only made Tanner angrier.

"You must be the little Ford," he said, sizing up Kevin with a mocking stare. "A Festiva, right?"

The crowd laughed at that too. Kevin just rolled his eyes. "Good one."

Danny glanced at Raven. She never took her eyes off him. He wasn't sure what her face was saying. Hang tough? Cut and run? All he knew was that he wanted to lose himself in those smoky gray eyes. But he couldn't. Not now.

"I could bust chops with you little guys all night," Tanner was saying. "But I've got a better idea. I say you choked at your tryout. You say you didn't. Well, prince that I am, I'm going to let you prove me wrong. We can play a game."

Uh-oh. Another wave of anticipation went through the crowd. They seemed to know what was at stake.

Johnny's eyes narrowed. "What do you mean?"

"Volleyball, my man," Tanner replied impatiently, tossing his hair back over his shoulder. "Here's your shot. You get to play the national champs three on three. Right here. Right now. In the dark for all to see."

Johnny glanced at Danny, then at Kevin. Danny knew what that meant. Johnny wanted to do it. No question. The line had been drawn.

Danny met eyes with Kevin. His younger brother's body was as tight as a wire. He gave Danny a subtle nod.

Johnny caught it. And that was all it took. He looked Tanner St. John right in the eye. "Sounds good."

Seven

THERE WAS A public volleyball court about fifty yards down the beach. When the Fords and the UC team marched toward it, virtually the entire bonfire party followed. It figured, Danny thought. Bloodbaths always drew a crowd.

"Just be cool and play your game," Johnny warned as they walked down the beach.

"That's great," Danny said under his breath, "but I thought we were supposed to play our game when the tournament started."

"The tourney's two months away," Johnny replied impatiently. "This is the perfect tune-up. We'll know what kind of a game these guys have. Plus we get some full-contact action. Like I said, perfect."

"Perfect except for one thing," Kevin muttered. "It's nighttime. I usually like to see what I'm hitting."

Johnny's voice was tense, as if his brother's comments were tiny annoyances. "They can't see either, Kev. Just be cool—"

"—And play my game. Yeah, I know," Kevin replied, shaking his head.

Someone produced a volleyball. The two teams batted it around to loosen up and adjust to the night. It wasn't as bad as Danny thought. There was a streetlight not far away, and the boardwalk provided a lot of residual illumination. Danny could see the ball well enough.

"Volley for serve," Tanner declared, punching the ball across the net.

Danny didn't mind. They were as ready as they were going to be in these alien conditions. He decided he would take Chevy Chase's Zen-like advice from *Caddyshack: Be the ball, Danny.*

He scanned the sidelines for Raven. At first he couldn't find her, and panic gripped him. Did she leave? She wouldn't leave without saying good-bye, would she? Or at least good luck? Not after the night they'd had. Volleyball meant a lot to him— Danny really wanted her to watch him do the only thing he could do well. Then he spotted her. Off to the left with Doberman and the others. Raven's expression was tense. Was she worried about him? A ripple of excitement ran through him at the thought.

Concentrate, he warned himself, stretching his cold muscles. *She's watching, so be cool, play your game, and don't worry about what she thinks. Just win.*

Wise words, he figured.

The UC team flubbed the volley. Arliss set up Tanner for a spike but totally misjudged the distance to the net. Johnny went up and pounded the ball into the sand on their side. The sound brought up ooohs and ahhs from the spectators.

"Our serve," Johnny said, puffing with pride.

"Don't get too excited," Tanner muttered, kicking sand.

Johnny retrieved the ball and flipped it to Danny for the serve. "Shove it down their throats," he whispered harshly.

Danny gripped the ball, squeezed it, got a feel for it. It felt cold in his hand from the night sand. The surface gave just enough for him to palm it.

"Okay, Fords," Tanner taunted, dancing back and forth on his feet. "School is now in session."

Don't think about it, Danny told himself. *Just be the ball.*

He tossed the ball up like he had a million times before, watched the light shape spin against the black sky, and slapped it toward the net. He made solid contact in the darkness, a straight serve. He would save his fancier serves for when he was warmed up.

The ball shot across the net toward the far corner of the court. At first Danny thought he might have an ace, but Shooter Ridge dove and popped the ball into the air for the save. Arliss Neeson moved in expertly for the set. Then Tanner stepped up and prepared to spike it.

He mishit the ball, sending it off the side of his hand. He cursed for the whole beach to hear.

Kevin picked up on the lame hit, letting it bounce up from his folded hands. Danny stepped in and set up Johnny, a move they had performed over and over again during practice. He didn't even have to think about it.

Johnny timed the ball, glided up to the net, and leaped into the air as if taking off. His long arm snaked out and hammered the volleyball straight down into the sand on the UC side. Arliss dove for it but never had a chance.

Point for the Fords!

Johnny pumped his fist. Danny and Kevin high-fived him. "See, they aren't so tough," Johnny whispered, breathing hard.

Few people in the crowd applauded since no one knew who the Fords were. But Danny distinctly saw Raven clapping, which pumped him up even harder. He paced back and forth, flexing his hands, waiting for the ball.

"One—nothing," Johnny declared, rolling the ball to Danny.

"Savor it," Tanner grumbled back. "'Cause it's the only point you're getting off us the whole summer."

Danny smiled and served again. This time he spun the ball. But he didn't get his best stuff on it, and it floated. Shooter picked up on it right away. He sent it to Arliss, who popped it to Tanner, who sent a rocket into the sand between Kevin and Johnny.

"Our serve, hotshot," Tanner said, demanding the ball.

Danny stared at him, wondering where he generated such power on his spikes. The ball had been a blur on that last one. He would've had trouble picking it up in daylight, let alone at night. He'd actually heard the ball sizzling through the air before it hit the sand.

That's why he's an all-American, Danny figured. *They were just playing with us on that first point. We could be in trouble.*

Danny was right.

The next ten points were an object lesson in guerilla-rules beach volleyball. The UC team worked like teammates should, setting and backing each other up and landing spike after spike into the Fords' sand. Johnny grew angrier with each passing failure.

Inside fifteen minutes the score was twelve to one.

The UC group clapped and cheered their friends and taunted the brothers on every point. They knew they were pasting the Fords. And they knew they were getting to Johnny. Everyone knew they were getting to Johnny.

He cursed, kicked sand, or silently stewed whenever the ball was tossed back to Shooter Ridge for the next serve.

Shooter announced the score and sent a frozen rope over the net. Johnny had to step back to save it, diving into the sand and popping it up in the air. Danny moved up and set the spike for Kevin.

Kevin timed it, went up against Tanner at the net, and tried to pound it. But Tanner charged in hard, sending an elbow into the net. It caught Kevin in the chest and sent him to the sand. The ball dropped on the Ford side of the beach.

"Our point," Tanner said coldly, staring down at Kevin.

Kevin didn't move.

Johnny and Danny ran to their brother's side. Kevin lay there, heaving. He'd had the wind knocked out of him, but he seemed okay otherwise. Johnny charged the net.

"What kind of a cheap shot was that, St. John?" he bellowed.

"It was a clean hit," Tanner shot back. "If the little boy can't take the hit, he shouldn't be on the court. And you know it."

Johnny pointed an angry finger through the net. "All I know is you have a reputation for this garbage. If we were in the tournament, you'd be penalized."

Tanner stepped up to the net, his long hair wild, a dark gleam in his eye. "Look around, pal. You see any judges?"

Johnny fumed. Danny could see he wanted to charge Tanner, but he held back. "You're scum, St. John."

"Scum with a loaded trophy case," Tanner replied with a snicker. "And I'll have your amateur little head on my wall in a few minutes."

Danny helped Kevin stand up. "You okay?"

Kevin nodded, shaking Danny off and rubbing his chest. "He caught me . . . right in the solar plexus. I feel . . . ugh . . . like you look."

Danny chuckled. Kevin limped to his position and signaled for the serve.

And the massacre continued.

At one point Danny glanced at Raven. Her friends had left the game to return to the bonfire. But she sat by herself on the sand, watching.

I must be real impressive, Danny thought, the pit in his stomach growing deeper.

Just then the ball sailed toward him. He hadn't seen it coming. He dove for it, but the ball skipped off his hand and hit the ground.

Johnny roared. "Come *on!* At least make the *easy* ones!"

Danny's cheeks grew hot. He knew he should've had it. And he knew why he hadn't. He tried to force Raven out of his head. Tried not to look at her.

Have to concentrate, he told himself. But he knew it was a lost cause. He could forget about Raven about as easily as he could even the score of the game.

In a few minutes it was over. The final score? Twenty-one to one.

They'd scored one lousy point against Tanner St. John and his all-American goons.

"Good luck in the tournament, kiddies," Tanner called to them as he rejoined his group. "If you're lucky, maybe they'll let you use the playground while the real men play for the money."

"Just try your cheap shots at that tourney," Johnny warned. "We'll see who the real men are."

"You talk like a volleyball player," Tanner said. "Shame you don't play like one. Now the whole beach knows why you didn't make the cut at CU."

Johnny was livid. Danny could see the veins and muscles working in his brother's neck and jaw. His fists were balled at his sides, and his breath came through gritted teeth. All they could do was watch Tanner and his cohorts make their way back to the bonfire, hooting and laughing the whole time.

Scott and Charlie approached from the sidelines and offered their condolences, for what they were worth. "How could you play in the dark like that?" Scott asked. "I can hardly see my hand in front of my face."

"The dark didn't beat us," Kevin replied grimly. "They just plain stomped us."

Johnny kicked the volleyball across the sand.

"Let's go," he ordered.

"Go where?" Danny asked.

Johnny gestured at the empty beach around them. "Home, moron! In case you didn't notice, we just had our butts handed to us. I'm not going back to any party after that."

Danny blinked. Not going back to the party had never occurred to him. Raven leaned against the far pole of the volleyball net, casually tracing circles in the sand with her toe. She looked great, and Danny felt terrible, and he couldn't think of anyone he'd rather be with right then.

Certainly not Johnny. Not now.

Danny knew what it would be like back at the apartment. They would sit up until all hours listening to Johnny overanalyze why they lost. Whether or not they had what it took to play with the big boys. Whether or not this whole summer tournament plan was a waste of time. Danny couldn't bear the thought. Getting creamed was enough. He didn't need his brother rubbing his face in it all night.

"Come on," Johnny growled, marching toward the boardwalk and home. Kevin, Scott, and Charlie filed in behind him.

But Danny stood his ground. He glanced over at Raven. He saw a smile grow on her face. He walked over.

"Yo, Danny," came Johnny's voice. "Where do you think you're going?"

"Nowhere," Danny replied. He looked at Raven and smiled back. "I'm staying."

"You have to be kidding," Johnny called. "You played like it was gym class in fourth grade. Your head was ten miles away. The fun's over—it's time to go home."

"We *all* played badly," Danny replied, resenting the implication that the loss was his fault. "Now I'm going back to the party to forget about it. I don't need to break down each point to know how bad we stunk."

"Maybe you need a brain transplant to get your head back in the game," Johnny suggested bitterly.

He gestured at Raven. "You were staring at the sidelines the whole time. It's time to show some team loyalty and get back to the apartment. Now. We have a lot to talk about."

Rage boiled up in Danny. He wasn't a dog to be ordered around. "No. I'm staying. Scott, Charlie, why not come with me? It'll be cool."

Danny's friends glanced at each other. "No, man," Scott replied. "We've had enough for one night. Why don't you come back with us?" Scott shared another look with Charlie. "It'd be cool to actually hang out with you, you know?"

More anger churned in Danny. Now his friends were giving him guilt trips? No. Correction. They weren't so much interested in spending time with him as they were in *not* spending time with *Raven*. He looked at her, waiting. Then back at his family and friends. If Raven was any other girl, Scott and Charlie would go back to the party. Danny knew it. "I'm staying," he said after a moment.

"I don't believe you!" Johnny cried. "Get your butt back to the apartment now!"

The anger in Danny finally spilled over. He couldn't take it anymore. "No! If you're going to go all major general on us now, John Boy, don't waste your breath. I'm not thirteen anymore. I don't take orders from you or anyone else."

Johnny took a deep, steadying breath. He looked like he wanted to pounce on Danny. But then he simply turned and walked toward the boardwalk without another word.

Kevin only shook his head at Danny and followed.

Scott and Charlie stood there, as if they weren't quite sure what to do. "Come on, Dan," Charlie said. "Let's go hang out at your place."

Danny walked over to his friends and spoke in a low, careful voice. "Guys, I really, really like this girl. I wish you two were at least interested in hanging out with her, but you're not. I know you drove all the way up here, but you have to understand."

"We do?" Scott asked, barely masking the anger in his voice.

"I'm asking as a friend, dude," Danny replied, meeting Scott's stare. "You don't have to like Raven. Not that either of you bothered to get to know her. But you have to understand that I want to be with her. That I want my two best friends to want to hang out with us." Danny gestured in Johnny's direction. "I'm not listening to him bark at me all night."

"So we have to do it for you," Charlie pointed out, folding his arms across his chest.

"No, you don't," Danny replied simply. "You can come back to the party with me and Raven."

Scott and Charlie looked at each other. Then Scott said, "No thanks."

He turned away and walked toward the receding figures of Johnny and Kevin.

"What about you, Charlie?" Danny asked.

Charlie shrugged. "Have a good time."

And Danny was left alone on the volleyball-court

sand. He watched his friends disappear into the night. He knew he should feel guilt, or remorse, or something negative. Maybe staying was the wrong thing to do. Maybe he should remain loyal to his brothers and teammates and friends. Maybe he should go sulk with them. But he couldn't.

Something else was driving him now. Something he'd never quite felt before.

Passion. Deep-in-his-gut passion. In the *I'm-dying-to-make-out-with-you* sense, yes . . . but more important, in the *I'm-dying-to-be-with-you, get-to-know-you, listen-to-your-thoughts, learn-your-dreams, share-my-own* sense.

Passion. The kind of feeling that gives you direction, that makes you *you.*

He turned back toward the party. The bonfire still burned.

And Raven was waiting . . .

Eight

DANNY AND RAVEN never made it back to the bonfire.

They ambled off down the beach in the opposite direction, toward the distant shimmer of the pier and amusement-park rides. The echoes of the boardwalk swirled around them. Music. Laughter. Bells ringing. It seemed a million miles away. The party still raged behind them, the bonfire reaching with orange fingers into the sky.

"Will your brother be mad?" Raven wondered, slipping her warm hand into his once again. "The older one, I mean."

Danny shrugged, liking the perfect fit of her palm. "Yeah. Probably. He gets like that whenever his ego is on the line. Or a lot of money. In this case it's both. He's banking on winning that tournament."

Raven searched his face. "Aren't you?"

"I guess so," Danny replied, kicking a clump of seaweed. "But honestly, I'm not thinking too far past tonight."

"Me neither," Raven said with a smile. "But sometimes you have to."

"There's that old worrying-about-the-future thing again," Danny declared, sighing. "I thought direction didn't matter."

"It doesn't, figuratively," Raven pointed out. "But you still need to prepare for the things that you can see coming."

"Such as?"

Raven shrugged. "Such as the fact that I'm transferring to a new school this fall and won't know a soul."

He squeezed her hand. "Why do you have to transfer?"

"My dad got a new job," she answered. "So we're moving." She looked at him forlornly. "I'm a little worried about fitting in and making friends—all that kind of stuff. You know how strangers act when they see someone who dresses like me."

Danny smiled. "Moving and going to a new school is a lot to deal with, Raven, but you'll do fine. I'd bet anything on it. And anyone who can't get past the look just has to talk to you for three seconds. You'll have no problem at a new school. Anyone would like you."

She looked into his eyes. "Your friends don't."

Danny dug the toe of his sneaker into the sand. He'd been hoping she hadn't caught that weird exchange between him and his friends. Or at least that the subject wouldn't come up. But he'd been stupid for thinking she'd avoid the issue. Raven wasn't the type to avoid talking about something just because it was difficult. She faced things head-on, uncomfortable or not.

And that was something he needed to learn from her. "That's exactly what I'm talking about," he said. "My friends didn't *talk* to you—they made a judgment based on the way you look, based on what they think they know of your crowd. It's wrong, Raven."

"Yeah, it's wrong," she agreed, running her hands through that silky brown hair. "But that doesn't mean anyone will give me a chance at my new school either. I'm okay with that—this is definitely who I am. And I don't go around worrying what people think of me—*obviously*. I just wish people would save their judgments till after they actually know me. Just because I'm comfortable with who I am and what I put out there doesn't mean it doesn't bother me when people judge me unfairly."

They were silent for a few moments. Danny had never had a conversation like this with anyone before. He'd talked music with girls. Television shows. Movies. He'd talked about classes, teachers, what kind of toppings he liked on his hamburgers. But he'd never talked about this. About life. Real life. Thoughts. Issues. He wouldn't have thought he'd be able to, let alone want to. But he seemed to be doing fine.

"You know, Raven," he said, brushing a strand of hair away from her eyes, "I have to admit something. I made a judgment on you based on how you look, based on you whizzing around on that skateboard. Maybe it's a similar thing to what you're saying, even if my judgment was a positive one. Maybe it's all superficial."

She tilted her head. "What do you mean?"

"I mean . . . the minute I saw you, I was sort of—" Danny paused, feeling his cheeks suddenly turn hot. He was grateful it was too dark for her to see him blushing.

"Sort of what?" she asked, a smile tugging at her lips.

Danny looked down at the sand, suddenly feeling shy. Raven gently tipped up his chin with her hand, her eyes questioning.

"Mesmerized," he finally said, his blush fading. "The second I saw you. I thought you were so pretty and so interesting. Just by the way you look, just by the way you dress, I decided you were this free spirit who knew exactly who you were, what you wanted, what you thought, and where you were going. I was attracted to all that. Everything I *assumed* you were just by looking at you. I couldn't get you out of my mind after that first night."

Raven smiled and knelt down to collect a palmful of sand. She stood up and let it sift through her fingers. *She's feeling shy right now too,* he realized, his heart pinging a little at that knowledge.

"And did the reality live up to the fantasy?" she

asked, letting the last of the sand flutter away in the night air. *"Am* I all that?"

He laughed. "You certainly are."

Raven froze. "Wait! I didn't mean it that way!"

They both laughed, and he took her hand. They continued walking down the beach, looking out at the water, up at the moon. Never before had silence felt so comfortable.

What is this strange connection I have with this girl? Danny wondered. *Why can I talk to her like this? Why do I feel so confident around her? Why do I feel like it's okay to be myself around her? She's nothing like me.*

Maybe you're asking yourself too many questions, Danny boy, he told himself as a perfect breeze swirled around them.

He squeezed her hand, and she squeezed back. *It's weird how much that says,* he thought. *A hand squeeze.*

He couldn't imagine anyone not liking Raven. Not wanting to be around her. Hear her thoughts. Hear her laughter.

But he wanted to be the only one who got to hold her hand.

"I'll bet every school has a rebel contingent," he told her. "Mine does, and the school you were going to obviously does. You'll find a new group of skateboarders to hang with. And you'll make friends in other crowds too."

"You're probably right," she replied. "I guess I'm just feeling a little nervous about changing schools. You probably didn't expect me to be Ms. Vulnerable, huh?"

Danny grinned. "Hey, just because you've got a friend named Doberman doesn't mean you don't have feelings."

Raven cracked up, and Danny couldn't help but laugh too.

"So where is this new school anyway?" Danny asked, sobering up at the thought of the summer ending. Of saying good-bye to Raven.

"The town's called Spring Valley," Raven replied. "It's about four hours from here. I don't know the name of the high school."

Danny stopped dead in his tracks. "Spring Valley High," he blurted out. He couldn't believe it. It couldn't be possible. Could it?

"How do you know that?" Raven asked.

Danny stared at her. "Because there's only one high school in Spring Valley. I should know. I go there!"

Raven stared back, her mouth slightly open.

"Are you sure that's the name of the town?" Danny asked, eyes narrowing. "You're not just messing with me?"

Raven shook her head. "How could I make that up? I didn't know where you were from."

"That is so weird," Danny said, his voice full of awe. "I mean, weird that we should meet now, the summer before."

Raven nodded. "It's a good thing. Because we probably wouldn't have met in the fall."

"What do you mean?"

"I mean what we've been talking about," she

replied. "Our crowds don't exactly mix. This is summer, Danny. And here, away from home, away from your friends, away from everything you're *supposed* to be, you can do stuff you wouldn't normally do. If we'd seen each other for the first time in Spring Valley, you probably wouldn't have looked twice at me."

Danny's expression said, *Yeah, right*.

"Well, okay, maybe twice," she agreed, surveying her clothes and rings. "But I don't think we'd be walking on any beaches in Spring Valley."

"There are no beaches in Spring Valley," Danny deadpanned.

"You know what I mean," Raven said, playfully punching his shoulder.

"Yeah, I do." Danny paused. "Maybe meeting you here and now is destiny."

"Maybe you're right." Raven met his stare head-on. "And maybe it's teaching us both some kind of lesson about appearances. If anyone had told me I'd be walking down some moonlit beach with a guy who shops at J. Crew, I'd never have believed it."

Danny laughed. "And Eddie Bauer."

Raven smiled. "Doberman's asked me why I like you. And when I tried to articulate it for him, I found it hard. I mean, I could say all the regular things, like that you're smart, you're sensitive, you think before you speak . . . you're really, really cute"—she glanced at him with a devilish smile—"but the actual feeling of why I'm drawn to you, why I want to get to know everything about you, is what I can't seem to put into words. It's just a feeling."

"A powerful feeling," Danny agreed, holding her gaze. He knew exactly what she meant.

In that moment he understood that stupid cliché about no words being needed. The feeling of understanding between them was so intense, it felt bigger than him.

Danny could hardly concentrate as he stared into those amazing gray eyes. This time it was he who tipped her chin up to him. She tilted her face, just slightly, and parted her lips, just as slightly.

And then he kissed her. Her lips were so soft and tasted faintly of cherries. Her smooth skin smelled deliciously like cocoa-butter suntan lotion. He wrapped his arms around her shoulders and pulled her closer to him.

Oh my God, he thought. *This has got to be what people mean when they talk about being in love.*

The very idea sent a shiver up his spine, and he pulled back. He felt nervous all of a sudden. Raw. Vulnerable. Exposed. Love?

Whoa.

He and Raven had something major going on between them, but Raven was right. This was summertime. This wasn't real life.

And she was transferring to his school in the fall.

"What's wrong?" she asked, looking at him. "Didn't like the kiss?"

Danny smiled. "Oh, I liked it. Big time. I guess

I was just thinking something. *At a really stupid time,* he realized. *Couldn't you have waited till after the most intense kiss you've ever had?*

"What?" she asked. "A kiss like that is supposed to be mind numbing. Whatever's on your mind has got to be big stuff."

Danny nodded. "Do you think . . . ," he began, but faltered.

"What?"

He shook his head, regretting that he'd opened his mouth. "Nothing. Forget it."

"What?" Raven asked again. She nudged him. "Tell me."

Go ahead, say it, he told himself. *Say it, and let the crumbs fall where they may.*

"Do you think we'll still be together then?" he asked carefully. "In the fall, I mean. When you come to my school."

Raven didn't answer at first, and Danny was sure he'd stepped in a hole. Then Raven shrugged. "Are we together now?"

"I hope so," Danny replied.

Raven smiled. "So do I."

Danny felt the butterflies in his stomach again, felt as light as the sea breeze in his hair. Not a bad feeling to have one week into the summer, he figured.

This time Raven kissed him.

They stood in the golden glare of the pier, arms entwined, Danny feeling nothing but the electric attraction between them.

He didn't have a thought in his head as she

105

deepened the kiss. Well, except for how beautiful she was. How amazing she felt in his arms. How comfortable he was.

She pulled away slightly, resting her head on his chest as he held her. "I have to get going," she told him. "I was supposed to be back a half hour ago. My brother's expecting me."

Danny nodded and held her tighter. They kissed again, and then he watched her jog away.

The loss of her presence hit him hard. Suddenly he felt chilly.

And this is the way it's gonna feel without Raven in your life, Danny told himself, shivering as he started back toward the apartment.

Despite how they felt now, Danny knew it wasn't a given that they would be together that fall when Raven joined him at his school.

He hoped so. But he wondered just how realistic that was. The crowd she'd fall in with at Spring Valley High would never let them live. There were Dobermans at his school, and that crew went around snarling down the halls at the Charlies, Scotts, and Dannys of the world. *Her crowd will never accept you or the two of you as a couple, Dan-o. So face facts.*

He crossed his arms over his chest as he continued on toward the apartment. *Or maybe it's your own crowd you're worrying about,* an inner voice challenged. *You know what your school is like. You know what your friends are like. You saw it tonight.*

So be truthful with what you're worried about, he

ordered himself. Which was: Could Raven be accepted by his crowd, by his family? And if not, was he willing to stay with her?

For the first time in his life Danny Ford went home with a twisting ache in his gut.

Danny awoke late the next morning. The other denizens of the rapidly deteriorating apartment had already risen, feasting on Pop-Tarts and handfuls of cornflakes. Danny blinked the sleep from his eyes, focusing on Scott and Charlie watching Bugs Bunny on the tube.

"Morning," he croaked.

Scott looked around as if a fly were dive bombing his head. "Did you hear something?"

"Nope," Charlie replied, stuffing pastry in his mouth, not taking his eyes off the screen.

Danny rolled his eyes and extricated himself from his blanket on the couch. He spotted Johnny and Kevin in the kitchen, improving on the mess of crumpled food boxes and milk cartons. He avoided their eyes. "Knock it off, you guys."

"What do you expect, Danny?" Scott demanded, finally tearing himself away from Bugs. "We drove four hours this weekend to see you. And we get maybe two minutes with you, a lame bonfire party, and a volleyball massacre. I mean, *yippee.*"

"If you wanted to spend time with your skate-rat girlfriend, fine," Charlie added. "But you could've told us so we didn't waste our time coming. Mike and Sherry were having a party this weekend, and we could have gone to that. We could have been meeting Sherry's cute friends and hooking up. But no, we drove four hours to see our supposed best friend, and then he blows us off for some really weird-looking girl he's known, like, a week."

Danny rubbed his face with his hands, hardly believing his ears. Yeah, this is what he needed first thing in the morning. "Oh, I get it," he retorted. "It's about Raven. My so-called girlfriend. Look, guys, the word *girlfriend* didn't even enter into the equation until after last night. I didn't expect for this to happen. And you shouldn't expect me to stop it. I told you that I really like this girl. Can't you be happy for me?"

Johnny made no effort to suppress his snort from the kitchen.

"I'm ecstatic for you," Charlie muttered. "Overjoyed. Elated. Hysterical. Look at me."

"Yeah," Scott added blissfully. "Maybe you and *Raven* can get matching tongue studs."

Johnny snickered from the kitchen. Danny then heard Kevin grumble, "Lay off him."

"You guys are hilarious," Danny declared, stretching and picking up a cereal box. Empty. He crumpled it up and tossed it in a random corner. "But I think I get the picture. You guys were great with the sorority types at the bonfire. But add a few earrings and some hair dye and a pair of tattered jeans, and suddenly a girl becomes too freaky for you. And I guess your bottle-blond dates from last year's Spring Fling dance—you know, the ones with more jewelry than the Home Shopping Network—they don't count, right? They're different, right?"

Scott and Charlie didn't answer. They just munched their food and watched Bugs.

"I don't know why you guys are being so weird," Kevin piped up from the kitchen table. "I talked to Raven last night. She seems like a cool girl."

Danny shook his head indignantly. "The problem with them is that they think *cool* and *girl* don't belong in the same sentence."

Scott snorted. "No, actually the problem is with *you,* Dan, and the fact that you've flipped over some freak. Can you imagine *Raven* at Mike's party? You'd walk in with her, and everyone would stop dead and stare. Sherry would probably watch her like a hawk to make sure she wasn't stealing anything. And everyone would probably be nervous she'd pull a knife or something or maybe that the rest of her freaky friends would crash the party—"

Danny had felt the blood draining from his face the minute Scott started on his little speech. "You're talking about someone I like a lot. So shut the hell up, okay?"

"Look, man," Charlie cut in, eyeing Danny. "He's being a little harsh. *Maybe.* But maybe you'd better wake up and face facts. Raven might be a nice person. *Might be.* But she looks scary, and so do her friends. You want to hang out with her, fine. But don't expect us to."

"You know what?" Scott said, looking from Charlie to Danny. "It doesn't even matter. It's a summer fling. She's different; you're attracted to her. Who cares? Once school starts, you'll be back home and you'll be into normal girls again, like Sherry and her friends. You'll forget all about your summer fling with the skate rat real fast."

Danny stared at Scott. Then at Charlie. Then at Kevin, who had one eyebrow raised at him.

Kevin's wondering if I'm man enough to deal with the fact that I like Raven despite all this bull, Danny realized. *If I'm man enough to stand up for the girl I like and admit to myself and everyone that it's not a summer fling.*

Suddenly Danny felt very uncomfortable. Very *examined.* He'd always thought it was Johnny who was testing him, pushing him, demanding stuff from him. But here was Kevin, his younger brother, expecting something too. Looking at Danny to do the right thing according to *Kevin's* standards.

Who do my brothers think they are anyway? Danny wondered angrily. *Why do I have to live up to anyone? Johnny wants to date an ice-queen cheerleader, fine with me. And let Kevin go out with a skate rat if he's so fine with it.*

"Let's get back to the point," Charlie said. "It's just a summer fling. And you've got the whole summer to have fun with your little skater chick. We're here one weekend. Hang with us like you know you're supposed to."

Danny let out a deep sigh. His brain was fried.

He realized he hadn't mentioned the interesting little fact that Raven would be going to Spring Valley High in September. Danny had enough trouble dealing with his own thoughts about that. He didn't need everyone else's opinion.

And he didn't want to have this conversation right now. What he needed was some breakfast.

Danny stepped over the floor debris—sleeping bags, pillows, tortilla chips, Fizz bottles—to get to the kitchen table. He found the box of Pop-Tarts—empty. He moved to the kitchen proper to search for more food. Johnny scowled, bumped his shoulder, and shoved past him on his way back to the bedrooms.

"Top o' the mornin', ol' bro of mine," Danny muttered, tossing another empty cereal box aside.

"Dude, that really is the point," Scott added from the living room. "We came to Surf City to see you, and we *haven't*. If you want to see Raven, fine. But tell us so we can pack up and go. End of conversation."

End of conversation. That was exactly what Danny wanted. To end this whole mind-twisting discussion and veg out. He was tired of talking about it, tired of thinking about it. Tired of wondering what the hell he was going to do.

Danny turned around and looked at his friends. On the one hand, they were right. He'd invited them up to the beach, then ignored them in favor of a girl. Which was pretty bad behavior.

"I'm sorry, guys," Danny said softly. "I did invite you up, and I have been ignoring you. So, how about we hit the beach for the day? Prowl the boardwalk. Hang out like always, and give this whole talk a rest."

Scott and Charlie eyed each other, as if deciding whether or not to forgive Danny. Finally they nodded. Relief flooded him.

Until he glanced at Kevin, who gave him a *whatever* look back before he turned his attention to his bowl of cereal.

Danny closed his eyes, let out a deep breath, and then quickly prepared for a day at the beach. Which pretty much consisted of changing into swim trunks.

As the three of them headed out, a single thought plagued Danny: *Raven's coming to my school in the fall.*

Had he let his friends off the hook because he was sick and tired of talking about it? Or was he using their objections as a way to put some emotional distance between him and Raven?

Come September, there won't be *any distance,* he reminded himself. *She'll be walking down the halls of Spring Valley High. Skating down the streets of your town.*

Danny sighed again as he closed the door behind him and his buds. These questions were way too heavy for the summer.

It was a beautiful day. The sun blared down on them, warming the boards and the sand. They soaked up the rays for a while and then wandered down the boardwalk to the pier, playing the occasional video game, eating some fries, and shooting the breeze. It was like old times between Danny and his friends. He even managed to push Raven from his thoughts briefly. Very briefly.

Until he saw her.

She skated up to them as they played a BB-gun game for baseball hats. She looked amazing in a black bikini top and beat-up sweat shorts that were spotted with paint. A towel hung around her neck, and her hair was wet.

"Hey," Raven greeted.

"Hey," Danny replied, watching Scott and Charlie for a reaction to her. They simply nodded, then stared at Danny expectantly.

Here we go, Danny thought. *Just say hi. That's all. I'm here with Scott and Charlie.*

"Where were you?" he asked.

Her cheeks were ruddy with sun and activity, and her smile just about pinned Danny to the wall. But he had to be cool. "We were on the water slide," she said, pointing at the massive coil of snakelike tubes that ran several hundred feet into a big blue pool. "You want to come? Doberman and the others want to get another hour."

Danny's smile evaporated. Of course he wanted to go. Right? But there were Scott and Charlie, BB guns in hand, their expressions asking him, *What's it gonna be?*

"I can't," Danny replied, hoping he didn't sound

angry. "The three of us have some stuff to do today."

"So why don't all three of you come for the hour?" Raven suggested. "It'd be really fun to get to know you guys," she added, looking at Charlie and Scott. "It'll be great. The water is perfect."

Danny quickly shook his head. "I don't think so, Raven. We really have some stuff to do."

Raven nodded. "So how about later? We could all get burgers or something for lunch, then go swimming."

Danny squinted up at her. "That sounds great, but I don't think we'll be able to."

She tilted her head and looked at him for a moment. "Oh. Okay." She took a step back, gripping the towel around her neck and bowing as if leaving a camera frame. "Sorry to bother you."

Something squeezed inside Danny's chest. He felt horrible but paralyzed.

No, Danny corrected. *Not paralyzed. You have a choice. And you're making it. Your friends came up to visit you, and you're going to hang out with them. That's the right thing to do, period.*

Isn't it? he wondered as he noticed the slight pink flush creep up Raven's cheeks.

"Look, Raven, it's just that Scott and Charlie drove all this way to hang with me, and . . ." He let the sentence trail off in the way he'd heard people do on television. He hated the way he sounded, like he couldn't just say what he really wanted. Like he had to imply what he meant.

114

"No, it's okay, Danny," she reassured him while simultaneously backing away. "I understand. Really. You have things to do." She dropped her board and stepped on. She offered Danny one last hurtful glare. "See you around. Maybe."

She pushed off and disappeared into the crowd.

"Raven—," Danny began, but she was gone. He cursed.

"What was her problem?" Scott asked, plinking a BB at his target.

"All you said was you were busy," Charlie replied, pulling another dollar bill from his pocket. "Chicks are weird, man."

Danny sighed.

What had he just done? Had he just ruined the greatest thing that had ever happened to him? Or had he done what was realistic for him? Sensible.

Johnny would be proud.

Kevin would shake his head in disappointment.

And Danny . . . what would he be?

Miserable, he told himself. *Because that's exactly how you feel right now.*

What I Will Now Look for
in a Guy, Revised

by Raven

1. Honesty.

2. Integrity.

3. Someone willing to stand up for what he believes in despite what his narrow-minded, jerky friends think.

4. Someone who doesn't think what I look like represents who I truly am inside.

5. Someone who doesn't blow me off because he's embarrassed.

6. Someone who . . . Oh, who am I kidding? I don't want to look for anyone new. It's those darn eyes.

Nine

THE WEEKEND PASSED, and Danny saw no more of Raven.

Scott and Charlie left Sunday night, seemingly satisfied that their friendship was not only still intact, but maybe even stronger than ever. Yet Danny sensed an underlying suspicion that they somehow knew Raven wasn't out of the picture. And that maybe Danny somehow resented them for what had happened between them that afternoon on the boardwalk.

Either way, his friends hit the road, and Danny returned to work Monday afternoon.

Not seeing Raven ate at him. He delivered his orders robotically, scribbling and serving and clearing without thinking. Strangely enough, he got none of them wrong.

But everything seemed hollow. He wished he could talk to Raven, try to explain what was going on in his head. Why he'd acted that way on Sunday afternoon. Why he hadn't been around the rest of the weekend.

So just call her, man. Call her, make a date like normal people do.

I've never even taken her out on a date, he realized. *Why is that?*

Danny stuffed his order pad in his apron pocket and headed for the kitchen, where the employee phone was. He picked up the receiver and prepared to dial Raven's number.

And that's when he realized he didn't know it.

He didn't know her telephone number.

He didn't know where she lived.

He didn't even know her last name.

Frustrated, Danny hung up the phone. *I've been so focused on how she affects me that I ignored who she actually is,* he thought regretfully. *I don't know anything about Raven. I don't know how it feels to look different from everyone else. How it feels to want to look different. How it feels to be moving from your town, from your friends, your school. How it feels to start over somewhere else.*

How it feels to have your maybe-boyfriend's friends judge you as unworthy just because of the way you look.

How it feels to have your maybe-boyfriend be too much of a wuss to deal with it.

But I do know what it's like to be judged based on how I look. And it's crap.

I'm such an idiot, he told himself. *I am superficial.*

"Hey, Dan man. Your tables are freakin'."

He glanced up to see The Skipster, another waiter, eyeing him as he wrote out a bill. Danny nodded, took a deep breath, and placed his orders, then headed back out to the floor.

Around five he took his break. He grabbed some fries and a Fizz and walked out of Jabba's to his usual spot on the bench across the boardwalk.

He never got there.

Doberman skated up and batted the food out of Danny's hands. It scattered across the boardwalk, forcing passersby to dodge. Rage boiled up in Danny. This was the last thing he needed. He was miserable, tired, and hungry and wasn't about to play déjà vu games with a psychotic skate rat.

"What is with you and fries, man?" Danny demanded, surveying his spilled dinner.

Then Doberman grabbed Danny by the collar, slamming him against the railing of the boardwalk. And Danny knew he was in trouble. At this section the beach was a dozen feet below.

Doberman's biceps bulged. Veins popped in his forehead. His teeth glinted in the sunlight. "Forget the fries, cupcake," he growled. "You're about to have a very bad day."

Danny gulped. "I'm already having one."

Doberman bent him back farther on the railing. The wood bit into his back, rubbing angrily against his vertebrae. Danny smelled day-old pizza and body odor. Beads of sweat broke out on his forehead. He blinked involuntarily when a drop ran into his eye. Terror gripped him when he looked into Doberman's eyes; he truly had no idea how far the big guy would take things.

"What are you doing?" Danny asked, his voice tight with panic. People gave them a wide berth, trying to ignore them. He was on his own.

"Normally I'd flatten you on principle just because you're such a dork," Doberman said viciously, shaking Danny. "But since you broke Raven's heart too, well . . . now I have an even better reason." He lifted Danny higher on the rail, pushed him out farther. He could see the beach below—and it wasn't soft enough. "Prepare to die, pretty boy."

"Wait a minute!" Danny pleaded. "How could I have broken her heart? We had one night together! I hardly know her!"

"Tell it to the crabs!" Doberman replied bitterly.

Danny struggled, but Doberman had several inches and a couple dozen pounds on him. If he didn't think of something fast, next stop was the sand below.

"Are you nuts?" Danny asked frantically. "You don't just toss people over railings, Doberman! I didn't do anything!"

"Oh no?" the big guy declared. "So why is she so miserable? Why is she crying? *Why is she even into such a monumental loser like you?*"

"How am I supposed to know?" Danny replied helplessly. "I didn't mean to hurt her. I swear. I didn't even know I hurt her until now." That was a lie, Danny knew, but he was about to get tossed off the boardwalk if he didn't come up with something.

"Come on, Doberman. You know the score. Why would I hurt her?"

Doberman paused, clearly frustrated. He obviously knew that tossing Danny over the rail wasn't really an option. And since his threats were no longer really frightening Danny, Doberman's options had dried up. But his rage had not.

Doberman let go of Danny. His feet clunked back to the boards. He sighed and straightened his shirt and apron.

"You make me sick," Doberman said, his voice lethally serious.

"Why?" Danny demanded, his own anger surfacing now that the danger was passed. "What did I ever do to you?"

"Nothing, stupid," Doberman replied, dismissing his comment with a scowl. "But she's, like, in love with you, man. And you're too dense to see it. Or you do see it, and you're too much of a loser to deal with it."

Danny froze. Raven was in love with him? *Me?* he wondered. He'd realized just a little while ago that he'd thought about Raven only in terms of how she affected him. He'd never even given a thought to how *he* affected *her*.

He'd never thought he had much effect on anyone, especially not an amazing girl like Raven.

Could she feel the same way about him? Was she feeling the same misery he was now—the same twisting stomachache, the moody tension, the need to be alone and miserable? . . . No way. There was no way Raven could feel so much for him. Be in love with him. "That's impossible," he whispered.

Doberman sneered. "I thought so too. I personally don't get it. I mean, *look* at you."

Danny ignored the comment. He was too fixated on the *L* word. "She actually told you that?"

"Of course not," Doberman replied, as if Danny had just made the dumbest comment in the world. "She'd never say it to me. But she does, Danny. Even if she won't admit it. I know her really well."

Danny was dumbfounded. His mind raced. He didn't know what to say. It was all happening so fast, so out of his control.

All he knew was how he felt. Deep down. No filters. Exactly how he felt. And he said so. "I think I love her too."

Doberman laughed in his face. "You're a moron."

Danny blinked. "What do you mean? Now what did I do?"

Doberman shook his head in disbelief. "What are you telling *me* for?"

Ten

AFTER WORK DANNY combed the boardwalk for her.

It was a useless gesture, he knew. It was now dark, closing in on ten at night. Surf City was huge and packed to the gills with people. If Raven didn't want to be found, she wouldn't be. It wasn't until Danny wandered down near Wayfarer Avenue that he had an idea.

He found the site of the bonfire party. Much of the burned wood had been cleared and the ashes plowed under the sand by cleanup crews. But it didn't take long to reach the jetty where he and Raven walked that night. And it seemed so simple to find her perched on the same concrete piling.

Yet there she was, almost as if she was waiting for him.

"Get lost, Danny," she ordered.

Or not, he thought.

Now that he'd actually found her, he realized he didn't even know what he was going to say. *I love you too?* Suddenly he didn't know *how* he felt.

Why is this so confusing? he wondered. When he'd held her in his arms, when he'd kissed her so intensely, he thought he'd pass out, when he'd looked into her eyes, it had all seemed so simple. There was just feeling. Now there was almost too *much* feeling. His, hers, and everyone else's.

"Can we talk?" he asked gently.

"I have nothing to say."

A wave pounded the rocks in front of them. Sea spray fell across Danny's cheek. He wasn't going to give up that easily. "Well, I do. Your friend Doberman came to see me."

"So I heard," she said with a shrug.

"He's pretty subtle," Danny said, attempting a lame joke. "But he led me to believe that I've hurt you somehow. If I did, I'm sorry. I didn't mean to. But I needed to spend time with my friends. They drove all the way up here to see me—"

I'm lying through my teeth, he realized. He *had* meant to hurt her. He'd meant to drive her away so that he wouldn't have to deal with it. Her, his brothers, his friends, and the thought of September.

"—and you were spending all your time with some freak girl," Raven finished, her tone bitter.

Danny paused. "That's not right. I was spending time with a girl I really like. But I had to spend time with them too. I mean, a guy needs to spend time with his friends."

124

Where is this bull coming from? he wondered. *Why aren't I saying what I really mean?*

Because you don't know what you mean.

But this is Raven. The only girl I've ever been able to really talk to. And here I am, saying the kind of crap I'd say to a girl I don't even like. Just tell her how confused you are. Then the both of you can talk it out.

"Then why didn't you just tell me that?" Raven demanded. "Why'd you act like you'd never seen me before? Like I was just some girl bothering you? Your friends don't like me, so *you* won't like me anymore—is that it?"

Danny looked down at the sand. "Raven, I . . ." He trailed off, unsure what to say. What *could* he say? She was right. But that wouldn't make either of them feel better.

"You made me feel like—" Raven stopped talking. Danny could feel her eyes on him. "You know what? Forget it. You can't handle it, Danny."

He glanced up at her. "Can't handle what?" he asked.

He knew exactly what she was talking about. But he needed to hear her say it. Needed her to let him off the hook.

Raven crossed her arms over her chest. "Can't handle direction after all."

Huh? he thought. *What's that supposed to mean?*

"What does direction have to do with this?" he asked. "This is about you and me and our friends getting in the way. My friends can't deal with you; your friends can't deal with me. And once we're in the same school, forget it. No one will be able to deal with us as a couple."

Raven glared at him. "First of all, Danny, this has *everything* to do with direction. It has to do with you feeling something and letting yourself feel it, no matter how wrong or right someone else tells you it is. That's called believing in yourself, following your own heart. But like you said, that's something you know nothing about."

Danny felt himself stiffen. He didn't want to deal with this right now. First he had everyone on his case about Raven, and now she was on his case about his shortcomings. Great.

"Oh, like you know me so well," he shot back. "We barely know anything about each other, Raven. I don't even know your last name. Did you realize that? I couldn't even call you because I don't even know your phone number or where you live."

"Gee, Danny," she said. "Maybe you could have asked. Or maybe it doesn't matter. Maybe all that matters is how we feel when we're together. You didn't need my phone number or last name to know exactly where to find me tonight, did you?"

She had him on that one. Danny stood there, his hands shoved in his shorts pockets. All he'd wanted was to make up, but . . .

Raven stared at him for a moment. "And second of all, we're obviously *not* a couple, so I guess you don't have to worry about what your friends think or how anyone will react to us in September."

Danny felt a stabbing pain in his gut. He *did* want

them to be a couple. Instead of fighting right now, all he wanted was to grab her in his arms and hold her. But what about tomorrow? What about September?

"Forget it, Danny." Raven shook her head and slid down to the sand. She scooped up her skateboard and brushed past him. "Let's just forget the whole thing."

Danny marched after her. "Yeah, well, maybe we should."

Raven kept walking. "I guess I was wrong about you. We *are* too different. You proved it yesterday. Your friends made you brush me off. And my friends helped. But you caved. You couldn't handle it. It's better we know that now before . . ."

Before we fall in love, he finished silently for her. *As if we're not already there.*

Wait a minute. This is really happening, he realized. *She's really dumping you. And you're letting her.*

"Raven, wait!" he shouted after her. "I don't care about our friends. I just want you."

Raven whirled on him, causing him to stutter step to a halt. "You're not listening to me, Danny." Her eyes glistened in the dim light. Her voice was desperate, as if she was forcing herself to speak the words. "You've already proved that what *you* want doesn't matter. It's over between us."

"Raven, come on," Danny pleaded, the lump in his throat making it hard to speak. "Maybe we just need some time to figure all this out." Just when he'd met the coolest girl ever, she was going to tell him good-bye?

Raven turned one last time. "No. *You* need to grow up." Her lips were quaking as she added, "Leave. Me. Alone."

She spun on her sandal and was gone.

Danny wandered the boardwalk for hours. It became very late. Finally he made his way back to the apartment. When he opened the door, he saw both Johnny and Kevin sitting in front of the TV. They looked about as happy as he felt.

"Are you dead?" Johnny asked.

"Huh?" Danny replied, hardly hearing him.

Johnny crossed his arms over his chest. "You better be dead because that's the only excuse for missing practice."

Practice. What was he talking about? Then Danny remembered. Volleyball practice. They had agreed to meet at the lighted courts on the King Street beach after Danny got off work. But Danny had totally forgotten it. He'd left work and immediately begun his quest to find Raven.

"Sorry, guys," he said, his brain still fuzzy. "I had a . . . well, it was a rough night."

"What happened?" Kevin asked, absently scribbling on a sketch pad. He hardly seemed interested in the answer.

"Raven dumped me."

There. He'd said it. Now maybe it could actually sink in. But Johnny's reply was like a bee stinging him awake.

"Good," he said.

Danny scowled. "Good? Good for you, maybe. It's what you wanted since the day I met her."

"Don't give yourself a hernia lifting the weight of the world, bro," Johnny replied. "You only knew the girl a week."

"Shut up, Johnny," Danny growled, slumping into a kitchen chair. "You don't know anything about it."

Johnny rose from his chair. "Oh, I think I do. I think I know how badly we tanked out in that volleyball game. I think I know how badly we need to practice. I think I know how this Rave chick has turned your spine to jelly. You're forgetting why you came here in the first place."

Danny nodded wearily. "The tournament."

"The tournament!" Johnny echoed. "Hallelujah, Kevin! He remembers."

"Your precious little tournament," Danny continued. "Your precious little trophy. Your precious little king-of-the-beach crown."

"Hey, dude," Kevin said, angrily tossing aside his sketch pad. "Get it straight. Your actions affect all of us. Johnny won't admit it, but we can't win that tournament without you. That is not meant as a compliment. It's a fact. And if you go off the deep end with some girl, then you better be prepared to deal with us."

Danny chuckled. "I've been dealing with you two since the beginning of time. What's another summer?"

Kevin stood up and approached his brother.

"I'm serious, Dan. Raven might be a nice girl. A great girl, even. I'm no idiot. I see through the pink streaks and the belly-button ring. But when it comes to playing and winning that volleyball tournament, all bets are off. There is way too much at stake, and I won't let you mess it up for us."

"So much at stake," Danny grumbled. "Gee, sorry. I wouldn't want you to miss out on that lifetime supply of Fizz Cola."

Johnny paced back and forth. "You know exactly what we're talking about. The money! The ten grand! We *need* that money, Dan."

"Ah, yes," Danny said, holding up a finger as if remembering an old joke. "Johnny's legendary greed rears its ugly head once again, dictating what everyone else must do to satisfy his quest for the almighty buck."

"Stop talking stupid," Johnny shot back. "You know the score. That money's a big key to all our futures. College isn't just a dream for me anymore. It's a fact. It's happening. I'm not going to work in a factory my whole life like Dad. My share of that prize money is a big start toward something. And I'm not going to let you screw it up over a girl." He paused, letting out a massive sigh. "I mean . . . I know you don't care about me or Kevin—"

"That's not true," Danny said, but Johnny spoke right over him.

"—and you don't have any real ambition toward anything else. But I know that you love the game. Don't you care about volleyball? About winning?

Don't you want to crush those all-American morons out there?"

If there was anything Johnny could've said to reach Danny, that was it. Danny knew it. Johnny and Kevin evidently knew it. But his brother might be too late. Because Danny heard the words, understood them, but felt nothing but the old ache in the center of his being. The heartbreak.

And that had nothing to do with money, v-ball, or victory.

Danny gazed at his brother. Johnny expected an answer. Danny wanted to give him one. The right one. He felt he owed his brothers that. But there was nothing there.

In the end all Danny could say in response was, "I don't know."

Eleven

T HE NEXT DAY at work Danny's luck didn't improve. He messed up three orders and dumped a bushel of hot wings on the floor. It was as if every planet was aligned against him. Every move he made backfired in some way. Everything he did ended badly, whether it was giving someone a hamburger instead of a cheeseburger or mopping up hot sauce with white linen napkins.

After Jabba chewed him out for that mishap, Danny just shook his head, sighed, and thought, *It's official. Everyone hates me. My brothers. Raven. And now even Jabba.* Though Danny doubted that Jabba liked anyone at all, so he didn't take it personally.

Then, to top off his day, Doberman sauntered into the restaurant.

Uh-oh.

Doberman was in his full glory. Ripped sleeves. Skater shirt. Torn cargo pants cut off at the knees.

The usual shark-tooth earring and evil look. His board in one hand and some cash in the other.

When he saw Danny, he grinned maliciously and shook his head as if to say, *You're a lost cause, pretty boy.*

Danny tried to ignore him.

The cashier-hostess, a pretty girl named Louisa (and the kind of girl Danny figured everyone would want him to date), met Doberman at the door, asking if she could help him.

"Two dozen wings to go," Doberman ordered, no doubt savoring the look of fear he brought to Louisa's face.

"One moment, please," Louisa replied, shuffling off to the kitchen to put the order in as quickly as possible.

Probably to get Doberman out the door fast rather than a concern for quick service, Danny figured.

Doberman leaned against the wall near the exit, admiring the looks he got from the other customers as if he didn't have a care in the world.

That's when Danny spotted Jabba.

The big man had seen Doberman come in and was moving toward him, slipping his big belly between tables. Danny immediately remembered Raven telling him how Jabba had banned Doberman, Skunk, and the others from his restaurant.

And now they were on a collision course.

Danny thought of warning Doberman, but there was no need. He caught a whiff of Jabba and rose to his full height as the owner closed in.

Doberman's eyes grew livelier by the moment. Jabba might as well have had steam whistling out of his ears.

"I thought I told you to stay out of my place!" Jabba bellowed, apparently not caring that his scream brought the entire restaurant to a screeching halt. Everyone—customers, cooks, and waiters—stopped what they were doing and watched.

"But I just ordered some wings," Doberman said simply.

"I don't care if you ordered filet mignon or franks and beans," Jabba said, jabbing a plump finger on Doberman's chest. "I don't want you punks in here, making the place look like a halfway house for junior-high dropouts and ex-cons-to-be. Out! Now!"

"But I just ordered some wings," Doberman repeated, same tone of voice, same delivery.

"Consider it canceled!" Jabba hollered. "You're banned. You don't scare me, kid. You're a loser, and I don't want you stinking up my place."

Doberman took mock offense, flashing his vampiric smile. "I'm insulted. It costs a lot of money to look this good."

"You got surfboard wax in those pierced ears of yours, punk?" Jabba asked, incredulous. He poked Doberman harder on the chest. And from the look on his face, Doberman didn't like it. "I said get out!"

"No," Doberman said, all mirth gone from his voice.

Jabba's eyes widened in their paunchy little sockets. "What did you say to me?"

"I said no," Doberman repeated, stepping into Jabba's face, staring him down. "I ordered hot wings. I have cash." He held up the money. "And I want what I came here to buy."

Jabba snatched the bills from Doberman's hand and threw them back in his face. "Your money's no good here. I'm not serving you a thing. I don't care if you have a hundred dollars. I want you *out*."

The arguing escalated, each one yelling louder than the other. Danny hung on every word until something shook his attention free, and he scanned the crowd in the restaurant. They were riveted. And they were clearly rooting for Jabba.

That figures, Danny thought. *Kick around the skate punk. He dresses mean, he looks mean, he acts mean. He's worthless, and he deserves to be tossed out on his ear.*

Danny had no love for Doberman, but he knew what was going on was wrong. Doberman just wanted some wings and had the money in his hands. And Jabba wasn't going to serve him simply because he didn't like the way Doberman looked.

I'll toss out any punk who comes through the door just on principle, Jabba once bragged. And he was making good on that promise.

But what galled Danny the most were the patrons. The restaurant was nearly full. Dozens of people stared in rapt anticipation at the heroic Jabba chasing off the evil skate punk polluting his establishment. Ugh, the looks on all their faces. Superiority. Contempt.

They're just a bunch of greased-up, sunburned piles of self-loving ego, feeding hungrily on heart attacks and fries, Danny thought in disgust. *And they have the audacity to ridicule Doberman for the way he looks.*

It was so wrong. Everyone judging everyone on how they looked. It had destroyed his relationship with Raven. It had destroyed his relationship with his brothers. And now it was happening again right in front of him. It made him sick. It made him angry. It brought every last vestige of rage to the surface in Danny.

Enough was enough.

Danny marched over to the counter where he picked up people's meals to be served. An unclaimed basket of hot wings was waiting there, steaming. Danny grabbed the plastic basket and headed for the front of the restaurant.

When he got to the arguing pair, he shoved the food between them. "Your wings, sir."

Doberman and Jabba froze in midsentence. At first Doberman blinked. Then a smile broke out over his face. He grabbed the basket of wings and stepped away from Jabba. "Much obliged," he said, laughing.

Jabba's face turned as red as a cooked lobster. He whirled on Danny. "What do you think you're doing?" he roared.

Danny didn't back away. He got right in Jabba's face and opened the floodgates to all of his anger.

"No, what do *you* think you're doing? This is a restaurant. This guy wants some wings. We serve them. He came in here and politely ordered some, and for no good reason, you tell him his money's no good. That he was already banned. And for what? For looking like a freak."

Jabba's eyes narrowed. He raised a porky finger at Danny. "How dare you tell me my business, you little twerp?"

"How dare me?" Danny asked. "How dare you! I stand in this restaurant every day, listening to you ridicule people. Like *you're* perfect. You ought to take a look in the mirror sometime. Does ragging on people make you feel good? Does it make up for something? Some personal lack?" Danny pointed at Doberman, who was happily munching on a hot wing and listening to every word. "What did he ever do to you, Jabba? I'm so sick and tired of people judging people by how they look."

Jabba's jaw was hanging open, and his jowls quivered with rage. "Get out. You're fired. Both of you punks get out of my restaurant right now, or I'll call the cops."

Danny quickly untied his apron and threw it to the floor. He took a deep breath, held it, and walked out of a restaurant that was so quiet, you could hear a french fry drop.

"Not bad," Doberman declared as he chomped on a chicken wing. "Not bad at all."

Danny glanced over his shoulder, pausing when

he saw the big guy behind him. The air smelled fresher outside the restaurant, mostly because of the greasy Jabba food but also because of the insane adrenaline pumping through his system. "That guy makes me sick," Danny muttered, for lack of anything more clever to say to Doberman.

The big skate rat rode his board slowly alongside Danny. Danny just marched along the semicrowded boardwalk, fuming. He didn't feel much like talking to Doberman, but he also figured he didn't have much of a choice at this point.

"I owe you one, Danny," Doberman declared, licking his fingers. "No one ever stood up for me like that before, especially not for a basket of wings." He smacked his lips. "Say what you want about Jabba. But his wings are the best in southern California."

Danny was still wired. He felt the words spilling over without his really thinking about what came out. "Unbelievable. I lost my job. And for what? I'm so sick of people and how they look. I'm sick of how I look. I'm sick of having no direction. Of having to *have* a direction. Everything is do this, work that, practice this, stay away from that. Auuugggh!" He gestured at the ocean, the sand, the girls in skimpy bikinis. *"I've had it with this place!"*

"That's the way," Doberman encouraged him. "Let it all out. You'll feel much better."

Danny stopped dead in his tracks. He glared at Doberman with no fear because he was beyond caring what anyone thought about him. He was a man with nothing to lose.

"You know what, Doberman?" Danny replied bitterly. "Why don't you just leave me alone? You do it too. You took one look at me and saw a loser. You did everything you could to discourage Raven from hanging out with me. Remember 'pretty boy' and 'punk-rock boy' and 'frat-boy-in-waiting'?"

Doberman nodded and smiled. "That one was my favorite."

Danny scowled. "Just get away from me."

Doberman pushed his board and caught up to Danny. "Hey, don't hand me that, man. Everyone does it. It's human nature. Believe me, I've ranted this rant a hundred times before, and I've gotten nowhere with it. All you can do is be yourself and let everything else take care of itself."

"That's a crock," Danny returned, walking faster. "I've always been myself, and just when I think it's getting me somewhere, Raven yanks the rug out from under me."

"Raven?" Doberman asked skeptically, the early evening sun glinting off his spiky hair. "Dude, Raven didn't do anything to you. You did it to yourself."

Danny whirled on Doberman. "No. That's not it. I was always myself with her. I never tried to be something I wasn't. But when you and your friends and my brothers and my friends started seeing things they didn't like, bam, Raven suddenly doesn't like me very much."

Doberman didn't answer him. He only shredded the last wing and dumped the basket in a trash barrel.

"Tell me I'm wrong," Danny challenged.

Doberman shrugged. "You're dead wrong. She filled me in a little on the convo you two had. You *let* her go, man. You couldn't deal with everyone being on your case. You probably figured what was going on now was nothing compared to how bad it would get in September, when she transfers to your school."

Danny swallowed. Doberman was right. He *had* been wondering what it would be like to have Raven at Spring Valley High. To see her walking down the halls—to see her in the cafeteria . . . maybe even to sit next to her in math class! And even though he didn't consider himself to be conservative, he was by association.

In Spring Valley, Danny palled around with guys who wore Tommy Hilfiger and Gap, who had short hair and no piercings and dated girls named Lauren and Jessica. Raven was the complete opposite of anyone he'd ever known, let alone dated.

Besides, his friends had showed their true colors—if he showed that he was still interested in Raven come September, who knew what would happen to his social status? He knew it was pretty disgusting of him to worry about something like that, but he was just being honest. And besides, how would Raven enjoy being raked over the coals every day simply because she wanted to be with him?

Danny sighed. "What am I supposed to do, man? Let everyone make us both so miserable that we end up making each other miserable?"

Doberman rolled his eyes. "You're an idiot."

Danny scowled at Doberman. "Now what?"

"Man, I hear a whole lot of whining," Doberman said. "But I ain't seeing a whole lot of fighting for what you want."

"Yeah, right," Danny said. "Raven doesn't want anything to do with me anyway."

"Let me tell you something about Raven, Danny." Doberman stepped on the end of his board and popped it up into his hand. He leaned it against a bench and hopped onto a railing, swinging his bare feet as if he didn't have a care in the world. "I've known her a long time. And she talks a good game, but she's a marshmallow inside, just like you and me."

"You?" Danny asked, smirking. "A marshmallow? Yeah, right."

Doberman spread his arms wide. "There you go again. Judging away on stuff you don't know. Just because I could rip your head off with my pinkie doesn't mean I don't get all choked up watching Hallmark commercials." He laughed at Danny's expression. "My point is this. Raven's a girl. And maybe she chased you in the beginning. But she isn't going to chase you anymore. You're going to have to do some chasing yourself now."

Danny sighed, watching the sunset over Doberman's shoulder. "I don't know, man. She chased me off pretty good last night. She made it pretty clear that I wasn't welcome. That I was a big loser for not being able to deal."

Doberman was quiet for a moment. Then he cleared his throat. "You said before that you were in love with her. Is that true?"

Danny didn't answer right away. He wasn't expecting to have a conversation like this with Doberman. *But Doberman isn't the guy you thought he was, is he?* Danny reminded himself. *He asked you an honest question, and the least you can do is give him an honest answer.*

"Yeah," Danny replied. "I am."

Doberman sighed and slipped off the railing. His bare feet hit the boards without a sound. "So do something about it," he said, flipping his skateboard onto its wheels.

Danny figured that was the highest compliment Doberman could ever pay him. The skate rat was giving his version of a blessing. "Thanks."

"De nada," Doberman replied.

"Do you really think I have a chance to get her back?" Danny asked.

Doberman offered a sly smile and clapped Danny on the shoulder. "Well, pretty boy . . . I'll see what I can do."

Twelve

"**Y**OU GOTTA BE kidding," Johnny said as he rose from his chair in front of the TV. An empty tortilla-chip bag fluttered to the floor. "Is this a joke?"

Danny had arrived at the apartment just after midnight. He and Doberman had roamed the boardwalk and beaches of Surf City all night. Danny felt like a huge weight had been lifted from his shoulders. He felt free, liberated. Doberman understood everything he was going through because the guy went through it all himself with his friends and family. In the end, Doberman was right. All you could do was be yourself.

Kevin's jaw dropped, revealing a half-eaten chip.

Danny chuckled and ran his hands along the bristly hair that remained on the sides of his head. Then he touched the field of angry spikes up on top. His new haircut would take some getting used to. Apparently Johnny and Kevin agreed.

"What, now I'm not allowed to get my hair cut the way I want to?" Danny asked, rolling his eyes.

"Yeah, if you want to look like a moron," Johnny replied angrily.

"Easy, Johnny," Kevin said, scowling. "It doesn't look that bad."

"What's with you anyway, Johnny?" Danny demanded. "It's more than just the volleyball. It has to be. Is it the late nights? Is it that I don't listen to you like you're Dad?"

Johnny didn't answer him. He just pointed to the fresh white bandage on Danny's bicep. "What gives?"

Danny grinned and gently tugged at the adhesive tape, peeling back the bandage to reveal a still-sore tattoo of a volleyball hurtling across his arm, streaking flames like a meteor.

"Whoa!" Kevin exclaimed, diving in for a closer look. "Cool!"

"Yeah, I like it," Danny said, beaming.

"Who drew it?" Kevin asked excitedly.

"The guy at the tattoo parlor," Danny replied. "You should see some of the stuff he did. He has pictures hanging all over the shop. It's incredible."

Kevin poked him on the chest. "Dude, why didn't you tell me you were going to do this? I could've drawn it for you."

"Sorry, Kev," Danny answered. "It was a spur-of-the-moment kind of thing."

Johnny only laughed, pinching the bridge of his

nose. "Well, now I can die happy because I've seen everything."

Danny let out a sigh, nodding. He'd expected this reaction from Johnny. In fact, he'd almost hoped for it. "Relax, Johnny. It's not your arm. You're still Mr. Clean-cut around here as far as I'm concerned." He'd tell Johnny when he was good and ready that the tattoo was a good fake. Doberman's friend at the tattoo parlor had drawn and colored it, and it did look like the real thing. He hadn't really wanted to do something that extreme—and besides, he wasn't old enough.

"Hey, heaven forbid if I offend," Johnny replied in mock terror. "I think it's really you, Danny. It looks great. Honest and truly. But I was just wondering when you had time to have all this art performed on you. After work?"

Here was the hard part, Danny knew.

He nodded, smiling. "Actually, yeah, it was after work."

"Did you leave early again?" Johnny wanted to know.

Danny smiled even wider, meeting his brother's stare head-on. "Actually, yeah, I did."

Danny could tell Johnny was running a slow boil now. "I see. And your boss just lets you come and go as you please? I thought that restaurant was superbusy."

At last, the moment of truth. "Actually, no, he doesn't. I quit. Or I was fired. It depends who you ask."

Johnny went absolutely ballistic. "I knew it! I

147

knew it! You idiot! You let all this rebel crap go to your stupid spiked little head!"

"Oh, relax," Danny said. "You'll pop a blood vessel."

Johnny's eyes went wide at the comment. His face grew more livid. "Relax? Are you kidding? Inside two weeks you've taken any trust we had in you, and you stomped it. What are you going to do now? Where are you going to work?"

Danny shrugged. "I haven't decided yet."

Kevin's face darkened. "Danny, that's not cool, man. How are we supposed to make rent?"

"Exactamundo!" Johnny cried. "Did you think about that when you staged your great walkout? Did you think about what you might be putting the rest of us through?"

"Yeah, I've thought about it," Danny said, nodding. "And I have a solution."

"Oh, I'm *all* ears," Johnny muttered.

Danny watched his brothers' faces carefully as he spoke. "It's easy." He paused for effect. "We win the volleyball tournament."

Johnny threw his hands into the air. "That's rich. You hear that, Kev? Suddenly Sid Vicious here is Joe Volleyball again. Uh, Dan-o? I have some news for you. You have to *practice* to be good at volleyball. To practice, you have to show up. You seem to be having a problem with that lately."

"Not anymore," Danny replied, confident.

Johnny blinked. "Not anymore. Okay. Good answer. I'm just supposed to take 'not anymore' and run with it after you shaved your head, stuck ink needles in your arm, and quit your job. Is that what you're saying?"

Danny shook his head. "What I'm saying is that I'm willing to do what it takes to win this thing."

Johnny straightened up, eyeing him skeptically. "Really?"

"Really," Danny confirmed.

Johnny took a step closer, focusing hard. "Are you willing to give up Raven to win?"

Danny's eyes narrowed. This was the challenge he'd expected. "Not a chance, Johnny. I don't see you giving up Jane or any of the things you're into. All I'm saying is that I'm ready to bleed to play ball. Just like you are."

"It's about time," Kevin replied, high fiving his older bro. "Good to have you back."

But Johnny shook his head angrily. "No, that's not good enough, Danny. All it took was one look from that girl to send you packing. She and her striped hair and Sex Pistols wardrobe have to go."

Danny had had it. Where did Johnny get off? Had Danny ever told him that his girlfriend, Jane, with her perfect hair and smile, her coordinated wardrobe, and superachieving GPA, had to go?

Danny looked Johnny straight in the eye. "Don't you see what you are? You dis people because of how they look. Are you so much better? Raven's grade-point average is near perfect. She reads books and listens to music you don't even know exists. And I'm through taking this garbage

149

silently. From you. From the world." Danny took a deep breath and sighed. "Maybe I need to try something different for a while. Maybe I need to see someone different for a while. I didn't realize how dead I was until I met Raven."

Johnny's scowl remained. But the savage tone left his voice. It wasn't a conciliatory manner, but almost exhausted. "Maybe you're right, Dan. Maybe I do make fun of people because of how they look. But people dress for that reaction. You could put a bone through your nose, but all you'd be is ridiculous. Different is inside, not outside. If punks and skate rats are so different, how come they all look alike?" Johnny slumped into a kitchen chair and crossed his arms. "The bottom line is, I don't need a brother with an identity crisis. What I need is a teammate who wants to play volleyball."

Danny smiled at the words and nodded slowly. He'd stood up to Johnny. In doing so, he'd stood up for himself. "Okay, brother. You got that. If you need proof, just check out my boss tattoo."

Johnny cracked a smile at that. Then laughed outright.

Danny grinned as well and offered his hand. Johnny shook it.

"It's always been the volleyball anyway," Kevin said, meeting his brothers' gazes. "It's what makes us brothers. We remember that, and nothing else matters."

Kevin put out his hand, palm down. Danny understood and was filled with relief that the three of them finally had it out. Danny was doing his own thing, and it didn't matter if Johnny and Kevin liked it or not. What mattered was that he didn't let them down in ways that did matter. Like the tourney.

But Danny knew nothing had changed between him and his brothers except the fact that they agreed to disagree. Which was fine with him. It was the best he could expect. He put his hand on top of Kevin's without hesitation. Johnny followed suit.

Now all he had to do was make things right between him and Raven.

But he had to find her first.

Thirteen

THE FORDS PRACTICED hard the next morning, slamming the ball around as if their lives depended on it. And in a way, they did.

Danny remained true to his vow. He concentrated. He dove. He was there in every sense of the word.

It was easier than he'd thought it would be. Raven remained in his thoughts, of course, but now he possessed a new focus. Danny had reached a turning point. It had happened when he'd stood up for Doberman in Jabba's. He'd realized that he believed in something quite strongly: acceptance. And that he had an appreciation for people's differences. Maybe that was why he'd gotten that haircut and the tattoo. To show himself and maybe everyone else that a spiky do and some ink didn't turn a clean-cut guy into a violent criminal. And the game mattered to him again. And that made it fun.

After their killer practice he showered the sweat and sand away at the apartment, then took to the boardwalk after his brothers left for their jobs at the Surf City Resort Hotel. He'd promised his brothers he'd look for another job—it wasn't fair to watch Kevin trudging off in his cabana-boy uniform and Johnny heading off to suffer with his annoying life-guard partner for yet another baking day in the sun while he was free to roam the beach and practice his volleyball serve. But he didn't want to fill out applications just yet. Right now he had more important things to worry about.

Correction: a more important *person*.

Morning sunlight flooded the beach. Instead of the loud children and parents dressed in even louder clothing who would be crowding the board-walk by midday, joggers pounded by. Walkers. Runners of every shape and size. They gave Danny and his haircut a wide berth.

He had to laugh.

Looks will always matter, he figured. *Fitting in is the hard part. A lot of people can't get past appearance. Look at Doberman. He's a real sweetheart once you get past the nasty shell. And Raven too. Well, I already know about Raven.*

That is, everything she wanted him to know. Danny knew plenty of things that mattered: like who her favorite bands were, what she really thought about life, how she liked eating cotton candy while skating the boardwalk. But he didn't know plenty of things that really mattered *now:* like where she lived, what her last name was, and her phone number.

"Duh!" Danny exclaimed out loud, causing the woman in front of him to turn around, startled. How could he have been so stupid?

I have to get Raven back, he thought.

It was that simple. Somehow. Someway. He had to do it.

As if on cue, Doberman rolled up beside him on his skateboard. Their eyes locked, a new understanding there.

"Dude," Doberman greeted.

"Dude," Danny replied, nodding.

"Nice hair."

"You too."

Doberman held up a crumpled piece of paper between his long fingers. Danny could see scribbling on it.

All Doberman said was: "Be there. Tonight at nine. The rest is up to you."

Danny snatched the paper from his fingers. Doberman skated off into the crowd. Danny uncrumpled the paper and read what was on it.

58 Arlington St. *An address,* Danny realized.

Raven's?

He'd find out soon enough.

Fourteen

THAT NIGHT DANNY had work to do. He figured it would take him about twenty minutes to walk to the address on the scrap of paper. Around eight he started to prepare.

He was still unused to hair maintenance. Spiking his hair was easy with hair gel; deciding whether or not he liked it was another matter. His hair wasn't that radical by some standards. He'd seen worse on some male models. He finally just left it alone, trusting what the barber—or rather *stylist* did to him.

The fake tattoo still looked great despite some tiny smudges from his sweat and the shower. The volleyball had been done in blue ink, the flames in red, orange, and yellow. Nice.

He chose a beat-up concert shirt from the Funeral Homeys, a thrash-rap group he'd seen live last year. The sleeves were short enough to show off the whole tattoo.

Now it was time to work on the jeans. . . .

Danny took them into the kitchen for surgery. He swept the crumpled fast-food bags and torn snack wrappers off the table to the floor. Then he spread out the jeans and took a dull butcher knife to them. A nip here. A tuck there.

Kevin wandered over and watched. "You want some artwork on those jeans?" he asked. "It'll take me ten minutes with a felt-tip pen. Might look cool."

"Nah, thanks anyway," Danny replied, focusing on his cuts. "I don't have time."

"Those holes won't look right until you wash the jeans," Kevin pointed out. "You should've thought about that."

Danny shrugged. "I didn't have time. I didn't know I was going anywhere until this afternoon."

"Where *are* you going?" Johnny asked from the living-room couch. "You look like you're dressing for the skate-rat prom."

Kevin laughed. Again Danny shrugged, taking the insult in stride. "I don't know. I was just given an address and a time. No other details."

"Sounds screwy to me," Johnny said. "You sure it's not a setup?"

"Setup for what?" Danny asked, eyeing his brother.

"Who knows?" Johnny answered. "Didn't this Doberman cat have it in for you?"

Danny shook his head, refusing to consider it. "No, this guy's totally cool. We made peace. My guess is Raven's going to be there tonight. This is my one last shot."

Johnny rose from the couch and joined them in the kitchen. He playfully tested the spikes of Danny's hair on his palm. "You sure that this makeover will help? She liked you before, didn't she?"

Danny knocked away Johnny's hand. "Maybe the makeover's not just for her."

Kevin smirked. "You mean it's for Doberman? Dan, I never knew. . . ."

"You're hilarious, Kev," Danny muttered. He flipped the jeans over his shoulder and tossed the dull knife into the pile of moldy dishes in the sink. Several fruit flies rose from the disturbance. "I meant me. Like I said, it's time to try something different. Maybe I'll like it. Maybe I won't. But I'll never know until I try."

"What about Raven?" Johnny asked. "What if she doesn't go for this whole punk-rebel thing? Then what?"

Danny shook his head. "I don't know, Johnny. I'll jump off that bridge when I come to it."

Johnny held up a hand and continued. "What I mean is, you made a promise to Kevin and me about the volleyball championship. It's the whole reason we came to Surf City in the first place."

Danny bristled. "Yeah, I know. So?"

"So . . . we need you to be a hundred percent into it," Johnny warned, obviously trying to word his remark carefully.

"What are you trying to say?" Danny asked, motioning for him to get to the point.

"A broken heart sucks the life out of you," Kevin blurted out. "If this chick stomps you, you have to remain human. That's what he means."

"Exactly," Johnny said, nodding. "No disappearances. No psychotic behavior. None of the stuff we saw all last week. *Comprende?*"

"Is that an order?"

Johnny chuckled. "No. We're just holding you to your word."

Danny nodded. Maybe Johnny had finally got the message about all the major-general-Dad stuff. Just like Danny got the message about the volleyball. "No problem, bro," he replied, walking toward the bedroom to get dressed. Then he turned back.

"I wouldn't worry, guys," Danny said. "My heart won't be broken for long."

"How do you figure?" Johnny asked.

Danny grinned. "'Cause I'm gonna win her back."

Fifteen

THE ADDRESS WAS south. Danny walked as far as he could on the boardwalk, enjoying the last of the dying day out over the water—a postnuclear glow of deep red where the sun went into the sea. The air was cool and breezy, the kind of wind that used to shuffle Danny's hair. Now his spikes just stood in the breeze like a petrified forest.

This will definitely take some getting used to, he thought, patting the crunchy gelled creation.

The boardwalk ended before he reached his destination. He took the street the rest of the way. As he walked, the houses got larger and more opulent. Huge postmodern structures with multiple levels, decks, and garages.

This is some big money, he thought. *Where is Doberman sending me?*

He got his answer soon enough.

The address matched that of the last house on

a dead end—right on the beach. The place was massive—a fantastic, slate-colored wood mansion with tall windows and decks of every size up and down the four-story frame. Danny could see dark figures on the decks. The pounding of a deep bass and voices filtered out the open windows.

"Big bucks," he whispered.

Danny made his way up a plank boardwalk to the front door. The house loomed even larger as he approached. The music grew in intensity. The laughter floated down from the glowing windows like an invitation.

Who lives here? he wondered, spotting a private-access path to the beach. *Someone's superrich parents, no doubt. This is a million-dollar joint.*

The front of the house faced the ocean. The double doors of the main entrance were wide open. A few kids near his age hovered there, soaking up the night air and laughing, talking. They ignored Danny as he walked right in.

He climbed a wide staircase to the main floor, a massive living room of expensive furniture and high-end stereo speakers built into the wall. He recognized the song immediately: "Miss Fickle's Pickle," a country spoof by the band Smog, a one-hit-wonder-to-be.

There had to be more than two hundred kids at the party. The crowd was mixed—girls in khaki shorts danced next to guys in shreds; guys in surf wear lounged next to girls in leather and studs.

Danny spotted Doberman chatting with two

gorgeous girls, preppies by the look of them. Maybe opposites really *did* attract, Danny thought.

When Doberman saw Danny, he immediately excused himself from the girls. He crossed the living room and bumped fists with him in greeting.

"How goes the battle, dude?" Doberman asked.

"This is pretty amazing," Danny replied, gesturing at the room, his eyes scanning for Raven.

"Thanks," Doberman replied casually. "I just put the word out, and people come. It's sort of like *Field of Dreams*. Kind of creepy sometimes. I'm thinking I should close the doors before things get out of hand."

Danny gaped at Doberman. "You live here?"

Doberman nodded.

"What does your dad do?" Danny asked, marveling at the cathedral ceiling and its huge skylights.

"He's retired now," Doberman replied. "But he used to be a plumber."

Danny blinked. "A plumber? How does a plumber afford a place like this?"

Doberman laughed heartily, clapping a hand on Danny's shoulder and pulling him close. "Dude . . . it's not my dad's house. It's *my* house."

Danny paused. "Say what?"

"You heard me."

Danny didn't know what to say. Could it be true? Was Doberman messing with him? "I don't believe it. . . . I mean . . ."

Doberman grinned. "Relax, dude. It's no big deal. I had to do something with my money.

Figured I might as well have a good time. I'm not really a yacht guy."

"How did you . . . ," Danny continued, still trying to make sense of it.

"You know the computer game Slob?" Doberman asked.

Danny nodded. Of course he knew it. Slob was the hottest PC game going last year. It was funny, disgusting, and superviolent like a great PC game should be. He owned a copy himself.

"I designed it," Doberman said matter-of-factly.

"You did?"

Doberman laughed. "What did you think I was, some kind of bum? I'm nineteen, for crying out loud. I have to have some kind of a life."

"I guess so." Danny chuckled, still dazed by the news. So Doberman was a multimillionaire computer-game designer. Unbelievable. "I guess looks really are deceiving, aren't they?"

Doberman winked at Danny. "Do tell, dude." Then he nudged him. "Don't look now, but I think your whole reason for existence is staring at you."

"Huh?"

Doberman pointed toward a corner. Danny followed his finger.

It was Raven. She was standing across the room, a look of disbelief and anger on her face. She stared right at him.

"Like I said before, Danny," Doberman said. "The rest is up to you."

Raven shot Doberman a look of death and disappeared into the crowd.

"Hurry up, dude," Doberman urged. "She walks real fast when she's mad."

"I know," Danny replied, taking off into the crowd after her.

He followed her down a twisting staircase to the lower floor. A massive sliding-glass door opened onto an elaborately decorated patio. Tiki torches burned at varying intervals, casting the whole area in a surreal island light. Raven was about to escape down a narrow path that led over a sand dune to the beach. Danny heard the pounding surf over the faded music from above.

"Raven, wait!" he called.

He didn't think she would. In fact, he anticipated another beach chase. But Raven actually stopped, whirling on him like the fabled woman scorned.

"When are you going to get the hint, Danny?" she growled, her eyes wild. "I don't want to talk to you." Then her eyes widened a little more as she took in his wardrobe and hair. A look of confusion crossed her face. "What did you do to yourself?"

"Do you like it?" Danny asked, feeling his cheeks get warm.

Raven sighed. "I liked you the way you were. Now go, Danny. Just go."

"No, Raven," he said, his voice rising. "I didn't just do this for you. I did it for me. Maybe you were the inspiration for it. But I realized I wasn't happy with who I was. I needed to change."

"You still don't get it, Danny." Raven shook her head, her voice weary. Even upset she looked totally hot: wild hair, smoky eyes, tight torn jeans, red tank top. Danny was just glad to see her . . . even if the feeling obviously wasn't mutual. "All you did was change your look. You can't change who you are with a haircut and arm art."

Danny nodded. "If that's true, then I'm still the same guy you rode the skateboard with that night on the boardwalk." He smiled. "Now I just have a killer tattoo."

Raven tried to suppress a chuckle but failed. This made Danny laugh as well—a breakthrough.

Go for it, the inner voice told him. *That little chuckle is your last hope.*

"I love you, Raven," he said, wording that momentous phrase with every ounce of sincerity in his body.

Raven shook her head, her voice cracking. "Don't do this, Danny. Just don't. It's too hard. We're too different."

Danny took a few steps toward her. He felt a floodgate open in his head. Words were flowing out in his mind before he even knew he was thinking them. But it didn't matter now. He had to say them. Because he didn't have anything to lose.

"Not anymore, Raven. I don't care what anyone thinks. It feels right. It *is* right. I'm not denying it anymore. I've been sitting around feeling sorry for myself too long. You're coming to my school in the fall, and I want to be with you. I'm asking you, please, if you feel anything at all for me . . . give me another chance."

A tear rolled down Raven's cheek. And it wasn't dyed pink or strange in any way just because it came from her. It was just a tear.

"What about your friends?" she choked out, wiping the tear from her cheek. "Your brothers?"

Danny shrugged. "They can find their own girls."

This made Raven laugh again. He smiled and risked a couple more steps toward her. She didn't back away.

"This is it, Raven," he said. "I can't put it any better. I'm putting it all on the line here. I need you. And I'm in love with you. I want to be with you and no one else. The rest of the world will just have to deal."

Her eyes finally locked on his. They glistened in the torchlight as she tried to blink back any more wayward tears. Then she stared at him. Shamelessly searching his eyes for something. *The truth?* he wondered.

After a few seconds she turned away, gazing at the beach, listening for something.

His mind raced. *Did I just lose her? Is she going to answer me? Or is she just going to take off again? I can't do this anymore. It's too much. I can't just spill my guts, tell her how I feel, and then hope that she says—*

"I love you too."

Danny blinked. Raven was looking right at him.

"You—You do?" he stammered, suddenly feeling woozy.

Raven nodded, a grin spilling across her face. She ran to him and wrapped her arms around his neck. Danny met her head-on, kissing her like he'd never kissed anyone before in his life.

All thought and sound fell away. There was just him, her, and the moment. He felt his heart pounding in his chest, in his ears, in their locked lips. It was a sensation he didn't want to end or to ever forget.

Then a gruff voice came from behind Raven from the beach.

"Awww, ain't that cute. It must be the tattoo."

Sixteen

THEIR KISS BROKE. Danny and Raven whirled at the voice.

A group of guys was coming down the narrow sand path in the dune grass. Some of them carried beer cans or smoked butts. But it was the guy in front who Danny recognized immediately: Tanner St. John.

His long hair was yanked back in a sloppy ponytail. His massive, lean frame was covered by a cotton sweater that hung loose from his broad shoulders. His tan feet sank into the sand with every step.

Then Danny noticed Arliss Neeson and Shooter Ridge behind him. Along with a dozen other guys who were obviously on a quest for a party.

"Well, well, well," Tanner said, grinning. "The freaks are out in force tonight." He leered at Raven. "You know, you'd be pretty hot if you took some of that dye out of your hair."

"Take a hike, frat boy," Raven muttered.

"Oooh, frat boy," Tanner replied in mock offense. "I'm touched by the poking finger of ridicule. Maybe you oughta get some staples for your lips too. Can anyone kiss you, or is it just Loser Appreciation Night?"

Danny felt adrenaline run through his system like molten steel. Rage built within him, bypassing every caution alarm that normally would have held him back.

But he was sick of holding back.

"Back off," he ordered, stepping between Raven and Tanner. "Take your act up the beach to the fun house. I hear they're short a clown."

Tanner and his friends burst out laughing. Tanner slapped his knee and staggered slightly. A few drops spilled from his beer can. "Oh, now that's a fresh one. You've been watching a lot of *Saved by the Bell,* haven't you?"

"Have another beer, frat boy," Raven scoffed, eyeing the half-crumpled can in Tanner's fist.

Tanner grinned. "You know what? You're absolutely right. Yo, beer dude!"

A can flew out of the darkness and landed squarely in Tanner's free hand. He popped the top and took a long gurgle. A tiny stream squirted down his cheeks. "Ahhh! The pause that refreshes. Okay, boys, let's paint this town battlefield red."

Tanner belched and marched toward the sliding-glass door. His posse followed like well-trained soldiers.

Danny stepped in front of him and planted a hand on Tanner's chest.

"I don't think you heard me the first time, dude," Danny warned. "I said get lost."

Tanner batted away his hand as if it were a fly. He stood to his full height—a good five inches over Danny—and glared down at him like he was now a serious nuisance. "I heard you, spiky," Tanner said angrily. "I chose to ignore you. Now get out of my way before something really bad happens to you. I mean *really* bad."

Danny smirked. "How bad is that?"

"Worse than your haircut," Tanner replied, sneering. "Now step aside. Or you'll find out what it's like to be danced on." He turned to Raven. "And *you* can be my partner."

The group fanned out behind Tanner, each of them larger than Danny, each of them primed and eyeing him like a fresh steak. Suddenly the high of winning Raven cooled off. The invincibility he'd felt was gone. Now Danny knew that it was just him against fourteen college guys who collectively outweighed him by one pickup truck.

He tried to remember everything he knew about fighting, which was very little.

Raven tugged his elbow. "Let's go, Danny. It's not worth it."

Danny knew it. Boy, did he know it. But something kept him rooted to his spot in front of Tanner. His mind said run. His feet said no.

If I back down, it's just one more victory for these

171

morons, the inner voice said. *Every time I see them, I'll know they got the best of me. I'll know that they can beat me. And I won't be able to do a thing about it. I can't back down. Not now. No way.*

"I'm not moving," Danny said flatly, staring right into Tanner's face.

"This isn't the volleyball court, little Ford," Tanner warned. "If you think it was bad out there, wait until I'm through with you. You'll think you dropped into the devil's backyard on laundry day."

Danny blinked and glanced at Raven, who shrugged. "What does that mean?" she asked, confused.

"It means I'm going to put you through a wringer and hang you out to dry," Tanner replied with a cocky smile.

"You make that one up yourself?" Raven asked in disbelief.

Danny refocused on Tanner. "If it takes fourteen of you to stomp my guts out, then fine, go to it. I can't stop fourteen guys. But remember what happens tonight because it'll all be squared on the volleyball court come tournament time."

Tanner roared with laughter. "Are you kidding? We beat you by twenty points in the dark when we were half wasted. What do you think is going to happen when we show up at that tournament with our game faces on?"

"We'll have to wait and see, won't we?" Danny replied, not a trace of fear in his voice.

Tanner shook his head. "Such a confident

young lad. Mama must be so proud." He flipped his wrist, spraying Danny with droplets of beer. "So what's it gonna be, tough guy?" He flicked more beer. "Are you going to move, or are you going to be moved?"

Danny ignored the drops of beer on his face and in his hair. He just took a deep breath and smiled. "Eat it, Tanner."

Danny batted the bottom of Tanner's can with his fingers, launching a healthy spray of beer right into Tanner's face. Tanner gasped, blinking as warm beer washed across him. A ripple of anger went through his friends as they waited for his reaction.

Tanner was livid. He tossed his beer can aside and clamped two hands on Danny's T-shirt, nearly lifting him right off the ground. "You're dead, Ford! Do you hear me? Dead!"

The group closed in on Danny, and he prepared to feel pain like he never felt before.

Then a voice piped up from behind him.

"Yo, Danny!" the voice called. "There are some people here to see you, dude!"

Tanner froze, leaving Danny to hang. Danny managed to turn around just enough to see Doberman, his vampiric grin flashing more wickedly than ever.

On either side of Doberman stood Johnny and Kevin.

And behind them about twenty skate rats of varying size, haircut, and rage.

"Hi, guys," Danny said lamely, waving.

Tanner dropped him. Danny backed away as Doberman and his crowd filtered out onto the patio, eventually flanking Tanner's group. Then surrounding it.

Johnny and Kevin moved in beside their brother. Danny felt new adrenaline flowing, the adrenaline of relief.

Doberman stepped into Tanner's face. "You were crumpling my friend's shirt. Explain yourself."

Tanner scanned the faces of all the skate rats. Danny saw weakness in his face for the first time. "It's our problem, pal. This has nothing to do with you."

"See, that's where you're wrong," Doberman said, scowling. "'Cause this is my house. Which makes this my patio. Which makes this my party. And as a gentleman host, that means I'm responsible for the guest list. Do you follow?"

Tanner nodded robotically. Danny noticed a drop of beer hanging from the end of his nose.

Doberman continued. "That means one thing. No scumbags allowed. Especially scumbags who give my honored guests a hard time. Guests who have earned the right to call me their friend." He shot Danny a quick, encouraging look. Then he got even farther into Tanner's face. "Do we have a problem with that?"

Tanner wiped the beer from his nose. Took a deep breath and licked his lips. "No. No, I guess we don't."

"Good." Doberman nodded, satisfied. "Now, pick

up your beer cans and get off my land. All of you."

Tanner eyed Danny and his brothers with contempt, then did as he was told. As he and his friends made their way back over the dune, he turned and pointed at the Fords.

"We'll be seeing you again," Tanner vowed. "Once you're on that volleyball court, you're fair game. We're not just going to humiliate you; we're going to hurt you. Mark my words."

"Looking forward to it, Tanner," Johnny called after him.

Tanner St. John only turned his back and disappeared over the dune.

When they were gone, a huge round of cheers and applause erupted from the skate rats. They high-fived Danny and Doberman, clapping their backs and making Danny feel like he was some kind of celebrity.

Raven stepped up and gave Danny a huge smile. "I can't believe you!"

"That I did so well?" he asked.

"No, that you were going to let them beat you up!" she said, giggling. She fell into his arms, and they kissed again. More hootchy-kootchy sounds rained down from all directions. Danny burst out laughing and broke their kiss.

Doberman then pulled Danny close and smiled. "You know what? You need a meaner haircut."

Seventeen

THE PARTY CONTINUED harder than ever. The guests were fired up, having seen the evening's entertainment. Doberman put on the Dustmites, and a mosh pit broke out in the living room. Danny and Raven caught up with Johnny and Kevin in the kitchen. Kevin was elbow deep in a bowl of cheese puffs. Johnny had already emptied a bag of pretzels. But to his credit, he'd managed not to spill many crumbs on the pale green tile floor.

"What are you guys doing here?" Danny asked. "How did you find me?"

Johnny shrugged. "We realized how lame we were being—"

"How lame *you* were being," Kevin corrected, reaching for a cracker from a tray on the kitchen island. "I was being pretty cool."

Johnny continued, ignoring him. "And then we got a phone call inviting us to this wild party at some strange address. It turned out to be Doberman."

"A party sounded pretty good at the time," Kevin added, hacking a hunk of cheese off with a plastic fork. "A good way to meet people."

"And a good way to make amends with our brother," Johnny added, offering Danny an apologetic smile.

Danny returned the grin. "Done deal, bro."

They bumped fists to make it official.

"Now," Johnny continued, standing and offering his hand to Raven. "I don't think we've been properly introduced. I'm Johnny. Danny's my loser brother."

Raven shook his hand, nodding. "I know. He is quite the loser. I'm Raven."

"So I hear you have a higher GPA than me," Johnny joked. "How is that possible?"

"I don't know," Raven said. "Maybe we'll find out this fall when I enroll at Spring Valley."

Johnny's jaw dropped. He gaped at Danny. "Is she serious?"

"Oh yeah, I forgot to mention that," Danny replied, his eyes twinkling.

"Sounds like destiny to me," Kevin commented, eating his cheese.

Danny and Raven shared a playful look. "I don't know," he said. "I think destiny is what you make it."

They walked out from Doberman's house onto one of the many decks overlooking the sea. Danny held Raven close, finally knowing that she wasn't going anywhere for a while. It was a wonderful feeling.

"So Doberman put you up to this?" she asked, gazing out at the waves pounding the shore.

"Yeah," Danny confirmed. "He thinks you're pretty special."

"I guess so," Raven said distantly, as if she wanted to avoid the question. "He can be pretty possessive."

Danny turned her toward him and looked into her eyes. "What is it?"

"It's nothing. . . . I . . ."

"What?" Danny pressed. "Is it Doberman? Did you two have a thing or something? He said he's known you for a long time."

Raven didn't answer.

Danny swallowed hard. "That's it, isn't it? He's your ex-boyfriend. Oh, that's just great."

Raven shook her head. "No, Danny, that's not it. It's like he tries to dictate everything I do just because I live here for the summer with him."

Danny couldn't believe what he was hearing. She lived with him? "What are you talking about, Raven? Why did you wait to tell me this?"

"What do you mean?" Raven asked, obviously confused. "Tell you what?"

"That you're shacked up with your ex-boyfriend, that's what!" Danny exclaimed.

Raven burst out laughing. Danny blinked. Now he was confused. "What's so funny?"

Raven grabbed him by the T-shirt and pulled him close. "Dobie's my *brother*."

Danny paused. Let it sink in. Recognition flooded him as her words finally registered. Then he started laughing himself. Raven kissed him through the laughter until they were quiet again, listening to the surf in the distance.

"So where do we go from here?" Danny asked softly.

"It's a long summer, Danny," she replied. "Let's just enjoy it."

Danny nodded, gripping her hand tight. "That sounds good, Raven. Really good." Then he leaned in close. "But I just have one question."

Raven's eyes were expectant. "What?"

A smile crept up Danny's face. "Your last name. And maybe Doberman's first name? And, um, your phone number."

Raven giggled. "Hey, you already know where I live. Isn't that enough?" She giggled again.

"You know what else?" Danny said, leaning closer. And closer.

"What?" she asked.

"You've already seen my tattoo. When do I get to see yours?"

Closer.

Closer still.

She gently pulled his head to hers, kissed him lightly on the cheek, and whispered a single word into his ear.

"Patience."

Do you ever wonder about falling in love? About members of the opposite sex? Do you need a little friendly advice but have no one to turn to? Well, that's where we come in . . . Jenny and Jake. Send us those questions you're dying to ask, and we'll give you the straight scoop on life and love.

DEAR JAKE

Q: *Do you think it's possible to fall in love with someone you've never met? I'm totally in love with the lead singer of a rock band—a really famous one. Even though I've never met him, I have seen him in concert and his songs make me feel like I know him. I'm trying to figure out a way to meet him, like getting a backstage pass. I don't want to date anyone at school, since I only want to go out with him. My friends tell me I'm being dumb. Am I?*

JQ, The Philippines

A: Crushes are never dumb. But, I think I understand why your friends are concerned. You don't want to date guys at school because you only want to go out with the rock star. But you've never met this guy, and chances are you probably won't! Enjoy his music, ooh and ahh at his face on a poster, go to his concerts and sing along at the top of your lungs. But keep in mind that it's his music and his image you love—not *him*.

Q: *Okay, I want the straight scoop: do guys only like blond girls with good bodies? That seems to be the case at my school! I have curly brown hair, freckles, and I'm not exactly a skinny-minny.*

MS, New York, NY

A: Okay, I'll give you the straight scoop: no! I, for one, being a guy, can tell you I like all kinds. The first girl I ever loved had curly brown hair, and she wasn't a skinny-minny, either. Sometimes it will be a smile that attracts a guy to a girl. Sometimes it will be her laugh. Sometimes it will be that she loves to read. And sometimes it will be her looks. Chemistry doesn't depend on a certain hair color or body type!

DEAR JENNY

Q: *My new boyfriend keeps asking me to wear makeup and "girlier" clothes, like skirts and dresses. I hate makeup, and I feel dorky in skirts. I don't want to lose my boyfriend, but I don't want to have to glop stuff on my face and wear clothes that make me uncomfortable, either. What should I do?*

DW, Baton Rouge, LA

A: You've hit on the keyword: uncomfortable. Doing anything that makes you uncomfortable, especially when you're doing it for someone else, usually just makes you *more* uncomfortable. Try telling your boyfriend straight out that makeup and dresses just aren't your style. If he persists in asking you to change your appearance, then perhaps you should think about changing your boyfriend!

Q: *My parents hate the guy I'm dating just because he looks tough and has a tattoo. I keep telling them that they don't even know him (they've only met him once for, like, a minute). Mike is the sweetest guy*

I've ever met, and I really like him. How can I get my parents to see past his "look" and realize he's a great guy?

AH, Dayton, TX

A: I suggest you ask your folks if you can invite Mike to a family dinner so that they can get to know him. If dinner seems too much, then perhaps you could all go somewhere together, such as a carnival or baseball game. Once your parents have the chance to see that he is a great guy, they'll probably be able to see past the "tough" exterior.

Do you have any questions about love?
Although we can't respond individually to your letters,
you just might find your questions answered in our column.

Write to:
Jenny Burgess or Jake Korman
c/o 17th Street Productions,
an Alloy Online, Inc. company.
33 West 17th Street
New York, NY 10011

Don't miss any of the books in
—the romantic series from Bantam Books!

#1 *My First Love* . . . . Callie West
#2 *Sharing Sam* . . . . Katherine Applegate
#3 *How to Kiss a Guy* . . . . Elizabeth Bernard
#4 *The Boy Next Door* . . . . Janet Quin-Harkin
#5 *The Day I Met Him* . . . . Catherine Clark
#6 *Love Changes Everything* . . . . ArLynn Presser
#7 *More Than a Friend* . . . . Elizabeth Winfrey
#8 *The Language of Love* . . . . Kate Emburg
#9 *My So-called Boyfriend* . . . . Elizabeth Winfrey
#10 *It Had to Be You* . . . . Stephanie Doyon
#11 *Some Girls Do* . . . . Dahlia Kosinski
#12 *Hot Summer Nights* . . . . Elizabeth Chandler
#13 *Who Do You Love?* . . . . Janet Quin-Harkin
#14 *Three-Guy Weekend* . . . . Alexis Page
#15 *Never Tell Ben* . . . . .Diane Namm
#16 *Together Forever* . . . . .Cameron Dokey
#17 *Up All Night* .Karen Michaels
#18 *24/7* . . . . Amy S. Wilensky
#19 *It's a Prom Thing* . . . . Diane Schwemm
#20 *The Guy I Left Behind* . . . . Ali Brooke
#21 *He's Not What You Think* . . . . Randi Reisfeld
#22 *A Kiss Between Friends* . . . . Erin Haft
#23 *The Rumor About Julia* . . . . Stephanie Sinclair
#24 *Don't Say Good-bye* . . . . .Diane Schwemm
#25 *Crushing on You* . . . . Wendy Loggia
#26 *Our Secret Love* . . . . Miranda Harry
#27 *Trust Me* . . . . Kieran Scott
#28 *He's the One* . . . . Nina Alexander
#29 *Kiss and Tell* . . . . Kieran Scott
#30 *Falling for Ryan* . . . . .Julie Taylor
#31 *Hard to Resist* . . . . Wendy Loggia
#32 *At First Sight* . . . . Elizabeth Chandler
#33 *What We Did Last Summer* . . . . Elizabeth Craft
#34 *As I Am* . . . . Lynn Mason
#35 *I Do* . . . . Elizabeth Chandler
#36 *While You Were Gone* . . . . Kieran Scott
#37 *Stolen Kisses* . . . . Liesa Abrams
#38 *Torn Apart* . . . . Janet Quin-Harkin
#39 *Behind His Back* . . . . Diane Schwemm

#40 *Playing for Keeps* . . . . Nina Alexander
#41 *How Do I Tell?* . . . . Kieran Scott
#42 *His Other Girlfriend* . . . . Liesa Abrams

SUPER EDITIONS

Listen to My Heart . . . . Katherine Applegate
Kissing Caroline . . . . Cheryl Zach
It's Different for Guys . . . . Stephanie Leighton
My Best Friend's Girlfriend . . . . Wendy Loggia
Love Happens . . . . Elizabeth Chandler
Out of My League . . . . Everett Owens
A Song for Caitlin . . . . J.E. Bright
The "L" Word . . . . Lynn Mason
Summer Love . . . . Wendy Loggia
All That . . . . Lynn Mason
The Dance . . . . Craig Hillman, Kieran Scott, Elizabeth Skurnick
Andy & Andie . . . . Malle Vallik

TRILOGIES
PROM

Max & Jane . . . . Elizabeth Craft
Justin & Nicole . . . . Elizabeth Craft
Jake & Christy . . . . Elizabeth Craft

BROTHERS
Danny . . . . Zoe Zimmerman

Coming soon:
Kevin . . . . Zoe Zimmerman

You'll always remember your first love.

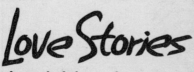